COLD STEEL

ISBN: 978-1-958051-79-5

COLD STEEL

JOYCE CH'NG

Snowy Wings
PUBLISHING

TURNER, OREGON

CHAPTER I

IT WAS SAID THAT the sword cut both ways and was as sharp as it could be blunt. That was why all the swordsmiths were sharp and blunt at the same time. It was also said that the Goddess of Swords, in a fit of rage at the complacency of the other gods, had broken the first blade with her bare hands, thus forming the tradition of sundering, where swordsmiths would break a sword to voice their displeasure at a decision made or intractability shown by the Council. Sliced by the shards, her blood had poured forth and made the River Veru and its tributaries. The great Yin t'Idan too had broken the Council Sword when the Council had proven unmoved by the pleas of the common fen people. She'd cried, "Our trust has been sundered!" and snapped the sword in two with her powerful, bare hands. Her blood had splattered on the floor. Until this day, the bloodstains remained to shame and mock the arrogance of the Council.

When Wehia Jirin t'Doniyat *ef* t'Tolani had left the t'Tolani holding, it had been justice she'd had foremost in mind. She'd too hidden something else, a secret shame. Wearing her blue robes, her Goddess-dedicated swords Cold Steel hanging by her side, Fire Heart strapped on her back, she wasn't the scruffy young woman who'd been seeking tutelage more than a year ago. Protected by her two blades, she wished for a brief respite of a hot drink and a warm meal. Mid-month of the Hook, her breath plumed white and her fingers were cold even in the gloves. They had left the City of Swords early in the morning. Beside Wehia, Geri Saara t'Dora *ef* t'Tolani, niece of Hadana t'Tolani, Wehia's teacher and forge mistress of the holding, shivered, pulling the blue headshawl across her face. Geri was Wehia's amal, her beloved. Courageous, her eyes bright, Geri now was pale with the chill.

What would the fens people think when they saw two figures, in colors of a prominent swordsmith holding? What would they think about the two swords that guarded one and the daggers that protected the other?

"Better to say we are ordinary travelers," Wehia said when they crossed the lake once more, the spires of the City becoming smaller and smaller in the distance. The ferry churned across the water. They chose not to cross the dangerous, swampy marsh areas, even though they were closest to the fens. Especially when it was cold and the bogs were surely freezing. Nervousness filled Wehia. The last time they'd been at the fens, they'd encountered soldiers who'd attacked a man.

"What ordinary travelers would bear arms?" Geri countered back cheekily. "We are not just ordinary travelers. Surely, many forge women have traveled this way before. They are used to seeing us. And there *are* bandits."

"I fought them off before," Wehia said.

"There you go."

"Go to the t'Nolyat holding at the edge of the border," Hadana t'Tolani had reminded them again before they'd left. *"They are our cousins and kin holdings, both t'Tolani and t'Doniyat. They will give you lodgings and food."*

The journey was not without its troubles. They disembarked at the jetty, weary of bone, dry of throat. They passed Fen Gorr, familiar ground they had crossed only months ago. They fought off bandits greedy for their coins. Wehia went after them with Cold Steel, not Fire Heart. Geri fought like a graceful cat slicing with sharp claws. The bandits fled. It was— for the most part—an uneventful journey and they had sufficient rest at the inns as well as food and drink.

They skirted past the t'Doniyat holding. Wehia's heart ached, longing for the warmth of her family hearth. She could see that her holding had not lit their signal fire. Justice burned in her heart, hot like the forge. She held fast to her purpose of finding out the cause of dissent in the border people. Her mother would definitely ask questions…

A secret shame burned too in her heart. Fire Heart was flawed. A tiny fracture marred its blade. She'd forged a flawed sword. Most of it had been her fault. Wehia had hidden the shame and embarrassment away. She was terrified of Geri's and Hadana's cold judgement. What would they say? She was such a failure. She was no forge woman. She pretended to be cheerful so that Geri didn't know. Wehia hated herself for lying.

What would her family think?

What would her *mother* think?

Better to keep on walking.

The t'Nolyat holding was a small manse at the border's edge. Nearby, a river ran swift and clean. Green was returning to the burnt land. It was burning when they first saw it, torched by fire and ash-choked. The trees were now covered with new shoots. Emerald curls of grass had emerged from the fire-darkened earth. Wehia saw sunbursts hung on the branches.

They felt like dried leaves: brittle and light. The border people had passed by here before.

Wehia felt sad. It was mid-autumn. The shoots would soon drop off when winter came.

When she and Geri approached the manse, they could see that it was all white brick and sturdy roof with ivy growing on the walls. A big chimney belched out black smoke, a sign of a busy forge. On the top of the roof was the signal-fire, glowing green. Like the holdings of the City, the fire was bright enough to be seen from a distance. Unlike the holdings of the City, the fire was only the signal-fire seen in the fens. Even the t'Doniyat holding had not lit their fire in this time of crisis. They didn't want to draw attention to themselves. It was odd that the t'Nolyat had lit their fire. But Hadana had said—and it was common knowledge—that the t'Nolyat were a mysterious clan who kept to themselves most of the time.

"Why did they light their fire?" Geri whispered.

"It's green," Wehia said. "The color of peace." Were they trying to signal that they were peaceful? "It's too quiet! I don't like it. "

She rapped out the complex code taught by Hadana on the solid,white door. Was it the correct code? Each forge had their own family code, their own personal language. Clans with kinship ties shared similar patterns like variations of a musical piece. To Wehia's surprise, a white-haired woman opened the door, clad in similarly white robes. The white was the color of snow. The color of the bone-steel people. Her eyes were dark. She looked forbidding and grim. The woman smiled and she was suddenly very beautiful. Geri couldn't control her reaction—she gasped, staring at the woman, clearly the forge mistress of the holding. She reminded Wehia of Hadana.

"You must be Wehia t'Doniyat *ef* t'Tolani and Geri t'Tolani," the woman said, her voice soft and measured. "We received the message from your forge. My holding welcomes you."

They stepped into a darkened courtyard with the light from the skylight filtering through and creating pools of murky white on the floor. Echoing out across the space was the clank and boom of the forge. Wehia walked past the holding's name plaque: a white crow with spread wings, its beak open as if it cried out in defiance.

"Forgive us for the dim light. Some of our sisters have sensitive eyes," the woman explained. "We wear protective eyeglasses when we work at the forge and when we are at leisure."

Women clad in white watched them silently while

they ascended the stairs to their rooms. Some of them had the pure-white hair like the woman. Some had pale hair, like fen flax. All of them had snow-white skin.

"I am Narin t'Nolyat, owner and forge mistress of the holding." The woman bowed gracefully when they paused outside their rooms. "Inside, you will find fresh water, simple seed bread, and our holding's cheese."

Their rooms were side by side. The corridor was torchlit but otherwise quiet. The t'Nolyat were a silent clan. While Geri washed her face, glad for the feel of hot water on her hands, Wehia picked at the sliced bread crusted with seeds and the sharp cheese, also pale of color but firm to the touch. The knives had handles made of fine bone. When she lifted one up, it seemed to shine with its own inner light.

Disturbed by the new environment, so strange and so unlike the t'Tolani holding, Geri slept beside Wehia, her hand tightly gripping Wehia's as if she were afraid to let go. She trembled in her sleep, troubled by dreams.

CHAPTER 2

WEHIA T'DONIYAT *ef* t'Tolani arose early, restless and unable to sleep. Instead, she took Cold Steel out and performed simple drills with it. Geri still slept, curled under the sheets. Her sleep was fitful. Pumps were working, flooding the courtyard with the soft, sonorous groan of gears moving. The forge was awake. It felt like Wehia was back at the t'Tolani holding. The same familiar sounds. She had to remind herself that she was not there anymore. The knife on the table wasn't t'Tolani steel nor t'Doniyat metal. It was bone. She knew nothing about bone.

She then slid Fire Heart from its scabbard. Blessed, Named, and Dedicated to the Goddess, it sang in her hands. The song was clear in her mind, a fierce fire that woke her senses and made her fingers tingle. Wehia was glad that Narin t'Nolyat did not question the presence of the two swords. All clans observed clan courtesy: what happened in one clan stayed within the confines of that clan. This also included the making of blades and other steel implements, their various styles and the reasons behind the making of each blade. Narin knew that Wehia and Geri were senior apprentices learning the craft from their forge. Wehia practiced the usual Figure-Eight drill with Fire Heart, delighted that it moved like a charm. The spirit within the sword sang to her soul. Fire Heart was still whole, wasn't it? No matter what, it was beautiful. *Her* sword.

Her mood lifted, Wehia donned the blue robes over the brown shift, for she was both t'Tolani and t'Doniyat. She left Geri still asleep, padding out softly. The corridor was silent, the torches lit. She expected to hear vigorous voices. Nothing. The t'Nolyat compound was completely without noise. Women in white drifted like ghosts. They moved in pairs or groups of threes and fours. Yet they neither spoke nor conversed with their companions. Wehia's robes were the only color that stood out, a strange echo of her first day at the t'Tolani forge. The t'Tolani forge women had accepted her as their own. The t'Nolyat women were a mystery. Even the legends surrounding this clan were intriguing. Descended from Riya, the third daughter of Lunes, they'd inherited her reticence and love of secrecy.

"They are an odd clan," Geri had said before they'd

slept. *"We are kin, but I don't see any resemblance!"*

"Bes and Yin were the more well-known forge mistresses." Wehia had nodded. *"They loved water and earth. Riya was the one who loved bone. Why bone?"*

A girl in white robes guided her to where they had their meals. Their dining hall was far smaller than that of the t'Tolani. The women ate in silence. The smell of the food stirred Wehia's stomach. At least she recognized the fragrance of morani stew. When she received the bowl of stew, it had bones in it: bird bones, fowl's bones, ribs, wishbones and chestbones. The stew, however, was piping hot and delicious, with hints of spice and molasses. She ate gratefully, picking the bones out carefully with her fingers. Women went around collecting the discarded bones. Silently, they bore them away wrapped in clean, white cloth. Where the bones went, Wehia could only guess.

Geri appeared, wrapped in her t'Tolani blue. The same girl led her to Wehia's table. She looked weary with shadows under her eyes. Wehia knew she hadn't slept well. When her bowl of stew arrived, faintly steaming and accompanied with fresh seed bread, Geri visibly shuddered.

"Why are there so many bones?" Geri hissed. "I hate this place. It makes my hair stand."

"It's only temporary. We won't linger here for

long," Wehia reassured her. Her neck prickled. "Eat this. It's morani stew."

"Too many bones. Are these bird bones?" Geri shook her head. She tasted the stew tentatively and proceeded to finish it, even mopping up the remnants with the seed bread. Wehia was glad to see that at least Geri was eating. She picked up her own utensil and finished the stew.

The same silence enveloped them when they went outside the t'Nolyat manse. Fog had rolled in, a blanket of fleece covering the earth and blurring the horizons. The line between river and borderland was hazy. While Geri looked wonderingly at the trails of ivy weaving across the white walls like intricate embroidery, Wehia walked up to the river. She could hear the rushing water. On the opposite shore was the land of the border people shrouded in the fog, just as mysterious as the t'Nolyat.

"Wehia!" Geri gestured urgently. "Look at this!"

Geri was pointing at something hung at the doorway, reminiscent of a wreath hung at various holdings' doors during the months of the Knife and Saber. The wreaths were to remind them of the time of planting and sowing, the time of promise. Wehia saw a sunburst, made of straw. Her heart turned oddly cold and she drew close to Geri, only to find that Geri had already grabbed her hands. She didn't let go.

They had seen those sunbursts before, hung on branches.

"What does this mean?" Geri whispered, a tiny catch in her voice.

"This means we are on the right path," Wehia said, giving her hand a tiny squeeze. "They will lead us to the border people."

Geri nodded.

Later, when the fog receded, fading away when the sun rose, they observed the women veiled in t'Nolyat white walking sedately to the river's bank with baskets cradled in their arms. It was not yet full sun. Their skin glowed. As they neared the bank, figures emerged from the river, wading across the water as if they were part of it. These figures wore straw hats and shirts. Indeed, their entire bodies were clad in straw as if they were beings of dry reeds and grass stalks. Their hands bore… large horns. Antlers from fen deer grazing in the fen forests. Small herds roamed the fens. She had seen them when she'd been growing up. The women bowed deeply and the items changed hands. The straw-clad figures bowed in similar fashion, the baskets in their arms. Silent was the exchange and silent was the way the women walked back to the manse, the big horns and antlers lovingly held as if they were ill children about to be nursed back to health. Wehia puzzled over the contents of the baskets. What was in them?

"We make handles, if you are wondering." A voice startled the two girls. They almost jumped. It was Narin t'Nolyat, a wry smile on her graceful lips. She held an umbrella in her gloved hands. The rest of her body was clothed in robes. She stood at the entrance of the manse. "And we trade with the border people. They find us bones and antlers. We give them food. It is a fair exchange."

Wehia flushed guiltily. Geri shielded her face with her head shawl, hiding her reaction.

"I know you are thinking, young Wehia and Geri of the t'Tolani and t'Doniyat. You think we are in danger by associating with the border people. Perhaps, you think we are dangerous too. Your aunt obviously thought so."

"No, no! I didn't mean it like that!" Wehia spoke and then closed her mouth, afraid that Narin would take offense.

"The matter is not as simple as it seems, Young Cousin." Narin beckoned them back to the manse. The two girls rushed back, glad for the silence. "Come," the forge mistress said and they followed her as she glided down the corridor. There was the sound of industry coming from their forge. It reassured Wehia. At least they had that in common. Narin brought them to her study, reminiscent of Hadana's study room back in the t'Tolani holding. *That* felt like a long time ago. There was a comfortable-looking armchair with plush, red cushions; a sturdy table of hard wood; and a large shelf filled with books. Their archives. Like the rest of the holding, the room was dimly lit. Narin lit a candle and placed it on the table.

"We are all kinswomen," Narin said. "Tied together by Lunes's blood. Water, earth, bone. We are stronger than we realize."

"What do you mean?" Geri asked curiously.

"That we would have stood united in the past, but sometimes our needs become more important than family ties. Come, sit, sit." Narin patted the seats next to her.

Wehia thought Narin spoke in riddles, but she didn't say so aloud.

They found seats on small footstools. Narin sat in her armchair like a regal queen.

"Your aunt was smart enough to send you to me,

to my holding. We can and will protect you from harm. The border people won't touch us—nor your own holding, Wehia t'Doniyat. That's because of a solemn vow they took a long time ago."

The two girls sat up straight, Wehia shocked beyond words, and Geri clearly feeling the same. Their mouths fell open. Wehia's heart pounded. Was she about to find out why there was such dissent amongst the border people? She placed a hand on her mouth. Were…Were the swordsmith holdings involved too?

"I suspect your mother and aunt haven't told you the full truth yet." Narin nodded, evidently unperturbed by their reactions. "Probably to protect you.

"We protected the border clans a long time ago. We took their side. The blood families didn't want it. They wanted to keep the hatred going. They wanted to lord over us. Ironic for people who rose to power because of their occupations. Many holdings rose up in protest, some more vehement and violent than others."

Wehia's heart beat painfully. She could see that Geri was on the verge of tears at the revelation. Narin smiled gently. "For a while now, all the forge mistresses vowed to remain silent on this. We dare not break the tenuous peace."

"Why?" Wehia asked softly. "Why?"

Narin didn't seem to hear her. "So, for now, we give them food. We have an understanding. It's the blood families' fault, not ours. The border clans' anger is directed at them, not us."

"But why? Why did they fight?" Wehia whispered.

"Because of pride and land they could acquire. It's hard to disentangle emotion and reason. The heart is a fretful beast, difficult to control. But you deserve to know the truth, young Wehia. Why would two scions of my kin holdings even want to brave the fens? I do not think it was mere adventure. Likewise, my cousin doesn't just do things without planning ahead. I gather you might have seen how the border people, the poor, and the downtrodden have been treated, young Wehia. You wanted to know what happened, didn't you?"

Wehia stared at her feet. Her boots had been stained dark brown by the long journey from the City to the fens. One single question burned inside her. The question that she had always wanted to ask her mother.

"What actually happened to my holding, Aunt? Why did we become makers of kitchen knives? We made swords in the past, didn't we?"

Geri flung a desperate, hot glance at her, shaking

her head vigorously. Wehia was about to tread on dangerous ground.

Narin merely smiled again, her teeth flashing white in the gloom of the study room. "Remember the legend about Yin t'Idan breaking the Council Sword?"

"Yes."

"This is a blood feud."

CHAPTER 3

"A BLOOD FEUD." Wehia repeated the words, feeling hot and silly for asking such a question. "What has the legend got to do with this? Legends are just legends!"

"Like Yin t'Idan, your great-grandmother protested against the ill-treatment of the border people. She fought an important lord from one of the blood families and won. The blood family was disgraced and embarrassed. As a result, they forced your holding to turn away from making swords ever again on the pain of death and complete dissolution of the clan."

Wehia gulped for air, unable to breathe. It was too much to take.

"Your great-grandmother was protecting the border people. She paid with more than her life. Her holding's honor was the price."

"But…*why?*" Wehia asked, knowing the question sounded more like a petulant wail. "Why did she have to do this?"

"She loved the border people. She said they were the same, like the blood. Flesh and blood. Mortal. They deserved to live peacefully. Like the rest of us. We are all the same. Of course, the blood families got offended."

Narin shook her head, catching her breath and regaining her composure. The forge mistress was angry. Her cheeks were flushed pink. Her hands clenched into fists.

"She challenged the lord to a duel. She used her best and favorite sword, Clarity. Everybody knew about the sword. Its fame spread far and wide. The lord lost because he was a poor swordsman with dismal skills. Your holding was still punished. She kept the sword, sworn never to use it ever again, and the holding became a maker of kitchen knives."

Wehia thought about Cold Steel and how it had been kept separate from the other blades in the armory. Was it… Clarity? Was she carrying the sword used by her great-grandmother? *Her* sword?

"Nobody from more than four generations onwards knows what Clarity looked like. It became history, a legend. The sword was kept swiftly and discreetly by Shani t'Neela herself. You should ask your mother."

"I did. She won't even tell me anything. Everything's such a secret." Wehia felt a hot rush of excitement. It pushed away the cold dread of knowing the truth of why her holding made kitchen knives. "I believe she doesn't even know about Clarity's make and appearance."

"Clarity must have been excised from your archives, then. What a terrible shame and loss. The sword was the only one of its kind. Very rare and very beautiful. There. I have told you about the reason behind your holding's current occupation. You hail from a brilliant and talented holding destined to make swords. You should not be ashamed of who you are."

"That's what Hadana told me." Wehia muttered.

"For your holding, the shame lingers and remains strong. Sometimes, shame doesn't go away. It seeps into the mind and paralyzes the person. It's dark, shame is. I wish the very best for your holding. We are kin."

Hot tears brimmed under Wehia's eyelids. It was more than she could bear. Shame on shame on shame. She didn't stop the tears from flowing. Sobs wracked her body. Geri placed a gentle hand on her shoulder. Her face too was wet.

When Wehia and Geri walked back to the main hall of the t'Nolyat forge, Narin having left earlier to give them some time alone, the tears had disappeared, replaced by a quiet, smoldering anger, enough to erase the shame of Fire Heart's flaw. Her holding deserved to have its name restored. She wanted justice for her family. Geri cautioned her against being too hasty, too angry.

"You can't just run up to the blood families and demand recourse," Geri said, her eyes flashing. She pulled Wehia to one side of the dimly lit corridor. "You can't be that impulsive. Stop it!"

"They wronged my family! My great-grandmother won the duel!" Wehia replied hotly. Her hands balled into fists. Geri saw that and frowned.

"You want to run away into the wilderness, just to fight with a blood family?" Geri said. "For what? To regain your honor? Your holding's honor? And for nothing again? If you want justice, you need to think and plan. Remember you are still an apprentice of my holding. Amal, you are a forge mistress in training, for Goddess's sake. What if you get killed instead?"

Wehia saw how much it took from Geri to speak like this and forced herself to calm down. Her heart thudded hard within her chest. Oh, her heart. Always angry. It needed to be tamed and caged. "I am sorry,

Geri. I… I just wanted my holding to regain its name."

"Remember why you are here, Wehia. Why you packed your bag and left for the fens. You said you wanted justice for the border people. Remember our original purpose!"

Wehia nodded slowly. Her heart became calmer. She knew where she was.

"Ask Aunt Narin," Geri said then and she began walking quickly towards the forge, where they were invited to help the t'Nolyat with their daily chores. "I bet she knows where to find them."

That night, the fog rolled in like a down blanket and Wehia watched the moon rise behind the thick cloud cover. It was quiet at the t'Nolyat holding. Nothing seemed to stir much. Not even a bark of an ore-dog or the thrum of the steam engines powering the holding. Geri had already fallen asleep. Wehia was so happy helping the t'Nolyat forge women, carrying their water, helping them watch the forge fire. It reminded her of home, she'd said.

Wehia leaned against the window ledge, staring out into the open. White wool covered the fenlands. It hovered over the river like a hesitant ghost. There, as she watched, balls of lights rose, one by one, slowly up into the air. They were far away. Were the balls of light lanterns? It was a fen tradition to send wish lanterns skywards.

Who was lighting these lanterns? And why?

Wehia watched the lanterns, glowing pink, until they disappeared into the clouds.

CHAPTER 4

Bone is fragile.
Bone is strong.
Shine a light
and bone is transformed.
- a traditional t'Nolyat children's ditty

WEHIA AWOKE TO the sound of children singing. It was early morning and the t'Nolyat holding had risen. Geri wasn't in her bed. The bedsheets had already been made, the bedclothes folded. Geri was a very neat person.

She found the t'Tolani girl with the holding's children. They were seated in a circle, right in the middle of the hall. The girls and one or two boys were smiling, their eyes shining in the dim light of the holding. They were singing about bone. When Geri saw Wehia approaching, she waved cheerfully. The t'Nolyat children got up, giggling, suddenly shy. Before Wehia could say anything, they ran back into the shadows.

"They taught me about their traditional songs," Geri explained, brushing her robes as she stood up. "They also showed me the bone knives they make."

"Bone knives," Wehia said. She'd seen some of them in the forge. They made them out of the antler and bones. In the light, they looked delicate.

"They are really beautiful. Just as exquisite as our knives and swords. I see similarities in styles and ways of making them," Geri said appreciatively.

"You are too kind." Wehia chuckled. She was hungry. Even the bony stew served by the t'Nolyat felt very appealing.

"They are our kin," Geri said. "And it's far better to be kind. The t'Nolyat are neither frightening nor aloof. Come, let's eat." Wehia wondered at the change in Geri's demeanor. She'd been so frightened when they'd first arrived at the manse. What had happened? Had she experienced a change of heart? But then, Geri had always been tender-hearted.

The morani stew was thick with fowl bone and crunchy cartilage. The two girls ate with gusto, mopping the flavorful stew with the fresh seed bread made by the t'Nolyat women. Then Narin came and brought them to the forge, where she taught them basic skills of making bone knives. For the other items they made for their patrons, they merged bone and steel together. The t'Nolyat called their blades bone steel, steel inspired by the resilience of bone.

"Don't look down on bone," Narin said, showing them a bone-white dagger. "Bone might look disgusting to you. To us, bone is life. Bone can be rough, smooth, jagged and supple. It can be shaped, like steel." Indeed, the holding's few apprentices worked diligently on filing pieces of bone just as the t'Tolani apprentices would on their wood and metal. Farther inside, the forge's furnaces glowed with the day's work of smelting.

Narin traced the dagger's tip across a piece of brown hide. The hide parted easily.

"We chose bone a long time ago. Bone serves its purpose," Narin said, placing the dagger back into its sheath. "This one is for a scion of a minor fen lord. It will help him cut meat and remove animal hides.

"If you shine a light under bone, it glows with its beauty," the forge mistress continued. She lifted one of the smaller antlers, still covered with a velvety layer, and hefted it, testing its weight. "This will make a sharp knife." She expertly sawed it open, exposing fresh marrow. Wehia recoiled. The strong, coppery smell filled the forge. The two young women wrinkled their noses. Brought up in forges of steel and ore, they hadn't encountered such things before. Neither had grown up with the smells of tanning leather that reminded them of sizzling bacon or the musty odors of bone and antlers.

"It can be as strong as steel," Narin explained as she sheared the antler down further with a sharp saw. "We make bone knives with the exact same principles as making steel swords and knives. Bone is not as porous as you think. If your bone is strong, the knife will not break."

"Like the heart of my sword," Wehia murmured.

"Yes." Narin nodded. "The same."

The two girls listened attentively as Narin showed them how to make a simple bone knife with the femur bones of fen deer. The steps were as rigorous as making steel daggers and swords. Apprentices took years to master these skills. Wehia tried her hand at polishing the bone. The process was long and arduous, and she couldn't stand the smell of the bone's edge rubbing against the hissing leather, even with the face mask Narin had given her. She would rather spend time in her own forge back at her holding or at the t'Tolani. The smell and taste of bone dried her throat.

The entire process was unbearable.

Belatedly, she realized what Narin was trying to teach them. When they shaped the bone, hers broke, because she was too hasty, too impatient. The bone cracked first before snapping in two and her nascent bone knife was ruined. Narin simply smiled and handed her another piece of raw bone. *Make a new one,* the forge mistress seemed to say. *You're not going to give up, are you?* Reminded painfully of that flaw in Fire Heart's blade, Wehia gritted her teeth and took the piece of bone from Narin's hand.

When Wehia emerged from the forge at last, her hands and arms aching, it was already late evening. Narin made sure the two girls finished making their bone knives, complete with wrapping their handles with deer sinew and tanned leather. Wehia still burned from the embarrassment of ruining her first knife. She had a long way to go. She needed to be more circumspect, less impulsive. She wasn't ready to be a forge woman. She just wasn't. Not when Fire Heart was flawed.

My shame. My secret shame. She flexed her fingers, a few tightly covered with clean gauze and smudged with spots of dried blood. Bone was sharp. It could cut through the gloves. She'd learned her lesson.

"These are beautiful." Geri admired her bone knife under the light. It glowed gently, the color of skin membrane.

Wehia stared at hers. Would it have been different if it had been Fire Heart instead? Would she have treated it differently? Would she have given up that easily?

Narin put the two girls to work at her forge with the rest of her women and apprentices. They carried water, bone, and wood from the supply room to and fro. They helped the experienced forge women with the bellows, nursing and sustaining the forge fire. After the afternoon meal, Narin taught them to tan leather. It was unfamiliar work, but Wehia and Geri soon grew used to the smell of fat and mashed animal brains the women smeared on fen deer hides.

"You smell delicious," Geri teased Wehia playfully. They were both eager to soak themselves in hot water. They stank, their faces covered with ash and dried animal fat.

"I never knew tanning smells like sizzling sausages." Wehia giggled.

The same routine repeated for two eight-days. Wehia and Geri became familiar to the rhythms and cycles of the t'Nolyat forge, how they rose in the morning, how they worked at the forge, and how they ate together at the dining hall. The t'Nolyat women had accepted them as part of the forge, since they were all kin.

They made bone knives, crafting exquisite scabbards for these blades under the supervision of Narin herself. They played with the children, teaching them nursery rhymes and practicing their letters. Wehia enjoyed all of these activities tremendously. They were all forge work, similar to what she had experienced at home and at the t'Tolani holding.

By now, the days had edged into the month of the Saber, the time of winter. Mere weeks were left before they had to return to the City of Swords. Wehia wondered if Narin was testing them. No matter how much she pressed Narin about the border people, the forge mistress remained tight-lipped. Wehia felt as if she were at the cusp of a major discovery and Narin was withholding more secrets.

Knocking roused Wehia and Geri from a deep slumber. They sat up, rubbing their eyes, sleep-soaked. "Who's that?" Wehia asked, yawning. It was not yet dawn and the forge was still, barring the soft rumble of the cog-work generators in the background.

"It's me, Narin." The voice was indeed the forge

mistress's. "Get up. It's cold. Dress warmly."

They wore their shawls and gowns, strapping their weapons on. Wehia opened the door to see Narin dressed similarly, her face covered.

"No weapons," Narin said firmly. Wehia reluctantly put Fire Heart aside. Geri frowned and removed her dagger.

"Where are we going?" Geri asked.

"It's time. Follow me," Narin said simply.

The air was frosty. Wehia often felt that the winter months were harshest and wettest at the fens. The manse was dark, lit only by the light of the signal fire. The stars were still out. They looked cold.

Narin moved on confidently, as if she knew where she was going. Wehia and Geri followed, their breath white against the darkness. They approached the edge of the river. It was there Narin paused. Wehia heard whistling, like the sounds made by marsh birds. A bright light flared up in the distance and rose steadily skywards. Wehia stared at it and found out that it was a wish lantern, its center glowing like a sun. She shivered. Something was about to happen.

Narin handed them two sunbursts made of dried straw. The sharp ends prickled the skin of Wehia's palm. "Hold onto them. They will grant you safe passage." Wehia and Geri nodded, wise enough to keep their mouths shut. Geri's hand shook in hers. A slight tremor ran through Wehia's body. It wasn't just because she was cold; she was also very scared. What was going to happen to them?

There was splashing in the dark. Figures with their faces covered with straw masks had crossed the river. Their entire bodies were clothed in straw. One of the figures lifted a hand and beckoned to them. The water was icy. Yet these figures seemed heedless of the cold.

"He wants us to follow them," Narin said.

Wehia inhaled slowly. Her heart throbbed. Geri held her hand tightly.

Together, they crossed the river.

CHAPTER 5

WEHIA, NARIN, AND GERI followed the figures in single file. They walked without the guidance of torches, their footfalls as sure as any fen-dwelling deer. Every dip in the brambled path, every bush and scrub, every thicket and grove, seemed familiar ground for the figures in straw. Wehia kept her eyes on Geri in front of her. Every breath she took felt like ice. The ground was soggy, waterlogged in some places.

Rustling about them indicated that they were being followed. There were many figures hidden in the bushes and shrubs. Wehia could hear more whistling. Another wish lantern rose in the air. It illuminated the immediate surroundings in flashes of light. Wehia glimpsed flocks of fen deer half-obscured by the sparse groves and more figures draped in straw beside the deer. The sky had begun to brighten with tinges of pale pink and orange. Wonder filled her.

Then everything turned dark. Someone had

thrown a blanket or a rug over her. It smelled like new animal hide. Shocked, Wehia opened her mouth to yell. She heard Geri shout her name.

"Walk," a male voice said. It was muffled by the hide. Wehia choked back tears of fright and anger. Had they been tricked? Had Narin led them into a trap? *Would* she? Wehia stumbled forward, shoved by a hard push on her back. "Stop that, Vex. They are guests on our land." The male voice again, stern this time.

Wehia obeyed. She sincerely prayed to the Sword Goddess that Geri was doing the same. It would do them ill if they bolted. They weren't armed with their weapons. They were also outnumbered. Her leg muscles shook with adrenaline. Wehia didn't like feeling helpless.

They seemed to walk forever. Thorn brambles brushed Wehia's forearms. She smelled tree sap, sharp to the nose, reminding her of fen pine, known for its aromatic oil. Fen pine grew next to her own holding. In the morning, the air was laced with its fragrance. Her booted feet sank into soft, dark loam. Where were they going?

Suddenly, they all stopped. Blinded by the hide, Wehia could only breathe through her mouth and count from one to twenty. She heard Geri's whisper: "I am all right." She glanced downwards. Wood sorrel with vivid-green, heart-shaped leaflets emerged from the matted layer of brown pine needles like intricate fretwork. How deep were they in the forest?

A woman's hand lifted the hide's edge and yanked it off. Light flooded in harshly and painfully. Wehia blinked furiously, trying to regain her composure. She saw Geri's wide eyes.

They were not alone.

They stood in the middle of tall fen pines. The trunks of the fen pines had been shaped by wind into twisted whorls, forming a natural bower. The air smelled of the wet, cold, dark loam and fallen pine needles. Honey-colored light lanced through the gaps in the archway of tree trunks, dappling the loam, coating the figures in straw with brownish-gold tones. There were more now, filling the bower with their presence. Narin stood with a figure who caught Wehia's eye because of their shortness. The t'Nolyat forge mistress had bared her face, showing it to the crowd. It felt like a bold and uncharacteristic move.

"Before we get things started," the short figure said. They spoke with the male voice Wehia had heard earlier, the stern voice telling off the one who had shoved her. "We meet in honesty." The figure removed the straw mask, shedding it. The rest of the assembly followed suit, peeling their masks and dropping them on the loam. It was a mixture of young and old people, both men and women. There were more women, Wehia noticed. Mostly older women. She stared straight at the short man.

Woman. Her dark hair was cut close to her skull. Her body was muscular, her arms sinewy, signs of hard physical work. Her face was tanned and lined. She reminded Wehia somewhat of Hadana. She had the same regal air.

"I am Mariad t'Ran, of the fens," she said. "I am the leader of this encampment."

"I am Wehia Jirin t'Doniyat *ef* t'Tolani," Wehia said, glad her voice didn't break.

Geri spoke up. "I am Geri Saara t'Tolani."

Wehia could see her shaking. She resisted the urge to hold her.

Mariad t'Ran nodded. "Lady Narin spoke to us about you. What do you want to know from us?"

"The truth," Wehia said.

A tall, stocky man stepped forth, his eyes blazing angrily. He held a short sword as if he wanted to stab her with it. "She's one of those accursed swordsmith women."

"Vex, stand down," Mariad t'Ran barked. The man subsided, but he remained sullen, like a looming thunderstorm. Narin appeared uncomfortable, shifting slightly where she stood.

"As you've noticed, my ancestry includes a holding, like yours," Mariad said. "My encampment is more diverse than just the holding ancestry, though. We accept all and reject none."

"Why do you set the fens on fire, then? Why do you hate the City so much?" Wehia pressed.

"We live on land that is for all," Mariad said without a hint of arrogance. "The fens belong to us all. Like the sun that shines above us."

That answer is too simple, Wehia thought. Why did the holdings even want to protect these people?

"We set the fens on fire because we want to send a signal to the City blood families. Destroy us, and you destroy the land."

"You get yourselves killed in the end," Geri said gently. "That's not good, either." The assembly of border people stiffened immediately. Were they offended by her words? *Oh, Geri, tread carefully…* Wehia thought.

Without warning, Vex exploded into action with incoherent roaring, rushing Geri, who sidestepped swiftly and kicked him hard in the groin. The man tumbled to the ground, doubling over, groaning in pain.

Geri calmly smoothed her robes and stood straighter, her face serene.

Mariad's face reddened. Angry? Embarrassed? "I apologize for Vex. He lost his father to a skirmish with a blood soldier regiment. Since then, he has harbored hatred." Her voice had softened. "We all lost many loved ones. Many in the encampments loathe the City for their arrogance and cruelty—"

"There are other encampments?" Wehia asked, her eyes widened in astonishment. "There are *more?*"

"Yes."

Wehia inhaled slowly. Of course there were more. The matter suddenly became too…complex, like a tangled ball of wire. Vex had ceased his dramatic rolling on the loam. He was soon back on his feet, glaring at Geri belligerently. Wehia knew in her gut that Vex would be a problem in the future. She stifled the chill that went up her spine.

"Tell me what you know about the feud between the holdings and the City," Wehia said. "Tell me what happened with my great-grandmother and my kin." She knelt before Mariad. "I can't speak for the rest of the holdings, but I can speak for my own holding. I am sorry."

"There's no need to kneel and no need to apologize, child," Mariad whispered, her voice huskier now with emotion. "Your holding protected us. We speak with honesty. Come, we will talk over bread and water."

"Our elders tell the stories during the moots." Mariad began talking the moment they broke hot bread and drank cold water. The border people had led Wehia and Geri to one of their campsites sheltered by the grove of fen pines. They'd been given loaves of dark, nutty bread the size of their open palms. Mariad had called them "palm bread," a food shared amongst family and friends. Wehia found the bread delicious, without grit or bits of flour. Palm bread was made from pine nuts and ground nuts gathered from the fens and then compressed before they baked them over fire. The fen pines produced thorny, brown cones the size of smooth, oval pebbles. The pine nuts were nutritious; they produced oil, which the women used. Wehia found the water refreshing and sweet-tasting. The border people were more self-sufficient and resourceful than she'd thought.

They sat on straw mats, heedless of the cold. Narin

joined them, sharing the meal. Other women made space for the newcomers. These women held important positions in the encampments: leaders of the hunters, the herb-gatherers, the seamstresses, and the herders. They wore simple clothing. Brown-colored fabric. Not threadbare, not tattered. There was a certain dignity about them.

"They speak of the lady who fought the head-in-arse lord and won fair and square."

Wehia had to laugh. "'Head-in-arse'?"

"They are often arrogant and think they are more superior." Mariad snorted scornfully. "Now, the lord wanted a piece of the land, not far from where we sit, and the lady said *no*. The lady was one of the swordswomen who guarded the fens. They made swords. The swordswomen watched over the fen and their sisters of the steel and blades joined them in solidarity. They truly served the Blade Queen, who protects the weak. The Sun Queen, who watches over us. You call Her 'the Sword Goddess.' She is one and the same. The fen people then were fen people, like you, forced to carve lives out of an unforgiving landscape. As generations passed, more and more people joined the fen people. The swordswomen promised to guard the fens. They swore that as long as they lived, the fen people would not live on the borders like drifting ghosts. The land was ours.

"The lord wanted the land for his hunting. He came with his hounds and his men. To the fen people, it looked like war. The lady knew about this and challenged the lord. She was a gifted swordswoman, talented with her blade. And what a blade it was! They said it could cut through steel. The fen people all watched the fight. The lord barely held his ground. He wasn't as skilled as she was. She defeated him.

"He was incensed! He went back to the City and wailed to the Council about the injustice he'd just suffered. Beaten by a woman! The Council believed him. So the swordswomen could no longer fight for the fen people. Could no longer protect us. They were forced to make knives. No more swords."

Mariad fell silent. She sipped water from her wooden cup. Wehia took some time to absorb the story. It all corresponded with what Narin had said.

Mariad continued. "The City soon forced the existing fen people to the borders. It was then we called ourselves 'border people.'"

"What about the sunbursts? I saw them too in the City!" Wehia said.

"The sunbursts are our votives to the Sun," one of the women replied. She was one of the older women, with a gnarled sun-browned face. "She protects us.

With it, you are protected from harm and given safe passage in our land."

"Some border folk use it as a symbol of rebellion," Mariad added. "'It's a symbol of anger, of strength. The homeless in the City have adopted the symbol, I heard. Anyone who has been ill-treated, ignored, and abandoned uses the sunburst as their cry to the Sun Goddess. There are some lords who have tried to stem its use."

They ate in silence. Wehia mulled over the story. She decided to speak up.

"The lady," Wehia said very slowly. "The lady was my great-grandmother. For a few generations, we've made kitchen knives. We no longer made swords."

An elderly woman cackled. "Reforge the Blade. That'll show 'em!"

"I can't just go up to the Council and take the Blade!" Wehia gasped, horrified. "That would be against tradition!"

The women laughed. Wehia felt as if she were back in the forge, with her kinswomen talking about their everyday routines or gossiping about news from elsewhere. Reforging the Blade didn't sound that scandalous. The Sword was broken for a reason: Yin t'Idan was furious at the blood families and saddened by the shattered peace. The physical brokenness of the Blade reflected the fractures between City and fen, between the blood and the border people. The problem went deeper and was more entrenched than just a few generations. Marching up to the Council to demand the Blade was indeed against tradition. More than that, it was suicidal. Yet…it gave her an idea. Wehia glanced over to Geri, who shook her head vigorously. To Geri, such an act was simply impossible. Without question.

"That's the story we know," Mariad said finally. "Passed down from our elders."

"Can I speak, Ma?" a soft voice whispered. Mariad nodded curtly. A young woman, about Wehia's age, had sat up straight. Clad in a light-brown tunic, her dark brown hair was pulled back in a rough ponytail. Wehia looked at her closely. She had seen those eyes before… And the memory of herself dropping the bread flooded back in.

"I met you before," the young woman said shyly. "It's the Sun Queen's will that I meet you again."

Wehia started, sitting up straight, her hand on her mouth. The border child!

"I am Kes," she said. "Mariad's eldest." She extended her hand in greeting.

"Well met again." Wehia reached out to touch her hand. Kes's hand was warm, her fingernails browned by soil. The world was small, indeed.

"Now I give you my open palm and bread." Kes cupped a palm bread on her other open hand and offered it to Wehia. "Well met."

CHAPTER 6

WEHIA AND GERI WERE later shown around the encampment. Mariad's leadership was obvious in the tidiness and cleanliness of the camp. Laundry hung under the sun to dry, flapping in the breeze like banners displayed on festival days. Women sat together, sewing and making clothing, repairing fishing nets, and grinding nuts for flour. The camp kept a small herd of cows and fen deer for their hides, meat and milk. They maintained a small shrine of the Blade Queen. The statue had the same features as the Sword Goddess Wehia had seen in the City's Shrine, but instead of white marble, the statue was made of dark, whorled wood. Despite the dampness, the camp was idyllic and peaceful, winter sunlight streaming through the fen pine trunks. The men were out, patrolling along the outskirts of the encampment as sentries.

Mariad's encampment was nomadic. Kes explained that they would only set up camp for a week or so before packing and moving to a new location in the fens. Their knowledge of the fens allowed them to find water and food. They lived on fenberries, pine nuts, tree nuts, fish, mushrooms, and wild greens. Their small herd of cattle and deer gave them red meat. The area close to the t'Nolyat manse was known to grow edible, leafy vegetables the border people called 'keffy,' which supplemented the encampment's diet. Keffy even grew during winter. Some border people, Kes said, also begged from travelers. However, begging was forbidden by Mariad. Curious, Wehia asked why.

"We live off the land," Kes answered quickly. "Others choose to beg." Wehia suddenly remembered the man whom she and Geri had helped. She wondered to whose encampment he belonged.

Kes explained that the different encampments had their own rules and politics, some looser in structure and composed of unrelated families, some more intimate and tightly knit with close family ties and connections. Mariad's encampment was linked to one another by marriage. An ally group was one led by a man called Heller, with whom they bartered for things like pots and utensils. An encampment generally respected the boundaries of the others in the vicinity, careful not to over-step the invisible demarcations and borders. *The border people have their own borders,* Wehia thought. *How ironic.* However, skirmishes between rival encampments were not uncommon. They often worried about soldierly incursions and attacks from their own. There were border people who chose not to live with the encampments.

"Sometimes, we set fires against each other," Kes said unhappily. "We fight amongst ourselves. There is no unity. The biggest, strongest encampments—Corwin's and Falia's—have always wanted to go to war against the City, with stolen weapons and all. It's a good thing that they were vetoed during the last Wintercold moot. Otherwise, we would be marching to war in the next Sunhot months. I don't like Corwin and Falia. They always set the largest and most destructive fires. Falia, especially. Her hatred is so great. Those two provoke the City constantly. They loathe the soldiers so much and carry out attacks on any passing regiment. As a result, the regiments always end up fighting back harder and bloodier. Some of our own people left to join these encampments too."

Wehia couldn't find words to say. It was strange. She'd thought that the border people had made up a homogenous community united under a singular goal or purpose. Why would people with similar beliefs fight against their kind? They fought against the same enemy! It shocked her to learn that two encampments wanted war. Why? Geri was also stunned into silence by Kes's revelations.

They passed a small group of boys practicing with wooden swords, their shouts ringing in the pristine morning air. Kes sighed wistfully, watching the boys with a look of wide-eyed envy on her face. Wehia knew that look. It reminded Wehia of when she'd been little, watching her mother with a practice blade. It was then that she'd pleaded to be trained by the holding's sword mistress.

"Do you want to learn some basic sword drills?' Wehia asked gently.

Kes's eyes shone brightly. "Yes, please, if you don't mind teaching me. Ma forbade me from learning the sword skills."

"She admired the swordswomen," Wehia said.

"Yes. But still she forbids me. She has her reasons."

They found sticks. Wehia taught Kes basic stances and guards. Geri instructed Kes how to breathe from her stomach and focus on her surroundings. Kes learned quickly. "It's not an overnight thing," Wehia cautioned Kes. Her old sword mistress had said the same thing to her a long time ago. She felt old. "You need practice."

During a brief rest, Kes turned to Geri and said

breathlessly, "You taught that swollen-head Vex a lesson! He was fast becoming trouble with his hot temper. Ma wanted to foster him out to Heller's encampment. He almost joined Corwin's crew. Ma stopped him and whipped his ass."

"Vex is your brother?" Wehia asked, surprised.

"Half-brother," Kes said. "I'm jealous of the holdings. I wish there weren't any boys or men. They're such a handful. Always angry and bitter."

"We welcome them back on festival days," Geri said quickly, her tone mild, as if she wanted to reassure Kes. She glanced at Wehia with some exasperation. "They have their good points and faults. They are still considered part of the clan."

"Skills are passed down from mother to daughter," Kes continued. "Ma tried. That's why you see more women and girls in positions of power. But we're not all descended from holdings. Some of the men protested a few years ago that the encampment wasn't a true holding and not bound to its traditions. Like we aren't a true sword or blade clan. Girls don't and can't use blades or knives to fight. Ma had to relent. She tried to placate the vocal ones in the encampment. I am afraid these vocal ones are winning.

"I see myself as a t'Ran. Like Ma. They were a small holding a thousand moons ago. It was said we made fishing daggers. The holding dissolved and the t'Ran scattered to the four winds. Some fled to the City. Most became border people. There were also women from your holding, Lady Geri."

"So I have heard," Geri said.

"Let's practice more," Wehia said quickly. She gazed back at the camp, where Mariad remained engrossed in an intense discussion with Narin. What were they talking about?

"I'm glad to find you again." Kes smiled, heaving her stick. She assumed one of the guard positions. "The woman's stance?"

"Yes, the woman's stance," Wehia said. She felt a sense of unease in her stomach. Should Geri know about her thoughts? Yes, she should, later, she decided. When they had some time to themselves. The more she learned about the encampments and about the border people, the more confused she became and the less confident. The matter was not as simple as she'd thought. Hadana was right. Geri was right. It was fast becoming extremely complex. She needed to review her plan again. Then again, had she had a plan in the first place?

Wehia and Geri were invited to share a meal with Mariad and the older women leaders of the encampment. The meal was comprised of fenberries, river fish, freshly picked keffy, and palm bread when the sun reached its peak. The meal was washed down with deer milk. Wehia thought it tasted like a barnyard, gamey and redolent of grass. She had earlier helped Kes gather the keffy and fenberries that sprouted in clusters under the fen trees and close to the stream. Kes had told Wehia that keffy was often eaten as a Sprouting green. *Spring greens*, Wehia thought. Spring was coming. Keffy had toothed light-green leaves that tasted sharp and peppery when eaten raw. In order to remove the sharp taste, the women tossed the leaves into a large iron skillet and fried them quickly with bits of fat. Keffy grew all year round. The fenberries were sour and sweet, a perfect end to the meal.

After the meal, it was time to leave. They had to return to the t'Nolyat holding.

"Hold onto your sunbursts," Mariad said when the meal had ended. "They will protect you. Other encampments will not hurt or harm you. Some of them are not like us."

Wehia and Geri bade the encampment farewell. Wehia clasped Kes's hands; the girl's eyes were red with unshed tears. Wehia wasn't sure when she would see her again. Vex, Kes's half-brother, was tight-lipped and moody. He stared coldly at Geri. Mariad and the encampment's women donned the straw robes, hiding their faces and their bodies. Solemnly, they escorted the visitors back to t'Nolyat land, crossing the river. Wehia thought, *That's our border that separates us from them.* The bog river of her home served the same function. *We create our own borders,* Wehia reflected sadly. *We are not that different.*

The straw figures soon melted back into a fog that had rolled in like a thick fleece blanket. Wehia's arms and feet were sore from too much walking. Narin led them back to the manse.

"I hope you have found what you wanted to know," the t'Nolyat forge mistress said.

Wehia pursed her lips. "I have more questions than answers."

"I am not surprised." Narin smiled briefly. "I suspected so. What would you do now, Wehia?"

Wehia heard Hadana in those words. Her teacher and aunt would have asked that too. She found that she had no ready answer.

"I'm conflicted," Wehia confessed to Geri as she collapsed on the bed, glad to have a soft mattress on her back. Weary after their visit to Mariad's encampment, they were glad to have the comforts of the bed and clean clothing, not to mention a long soak in the hot tubs prepared by the t'Nolyat women. Wehia was keenly aware of how fortunate she was.

Geri stretched luxuriously, dressed in a loose t'Nolyat shift as their soiled clothes were being washed in the forge's laundry. "Conflicted is an understatement," she said. "The matter's far more complex than we realized. They fight with other encampments too. They are not even united!"

Wehia sighed long and deep. "I don't know what to tell your aunt. I don't know anymore. Maybe I was too hasty, after all."

"And I don't think you could just march up to the Council and repair the Sword." Geri shook her head sadly. "That would be extremely foolhardy and dangerous. The blood families guard the shattered Sword."

"But the broken Sword means we remain broken too! A shattered people. City against the border people… against the fens. Oh, why is this so difficult?" Wehia sighed again.

"Their feelings run deep, blood-deep. I don't think you can just repair this rift like you do with a broken blade."

"I know, I know! I can't go back without answers,

without a plan. Your aunt—"

"—will understand. You can't solve the injustice without getting to the root of the problem. And this has entangled roots."

"I'm still conflicted! I feel very strongly about helping the border people…"

"They're in different encampments with different beliefs and goals, Wehia. Didn't Kes say that two wanted to attack the City? If you mean by 'helping the border people', do you mean all of them? Not just Mariad and her encampment? And would they accept your help?"

"Some of the women came from the holdings…"

"That was a long time ago."

"We have to return in a few days' time. I hate to go back without a proper answer. What will Hadana say?"

"I told you she would understand."

"And my holding's reputation! I want us to make swords again!"

Geri sat up from her bed. "Breathe, Wehia."

"It's not *your* holding that was forbidden to make swords!" Once the words came out from her mouth, Wehia immediately regretted speaking them aloud. Geri drew back, her cheeks flushed.

"I'm sorry." Wehia held Geri's hands gently. "I'm

angry… But at least, I know the reason why the t'Doniyat are making kitchen knives."

"Promise me you're not going to challenge them, the blood family that did that to your holding! And we don't even know which blood family! Could be any one of them in the City. They are all *that* arrogant…" Geri squeezed Wehia's fingers back reassuringly. "And promise me not to march up to your mother…"

They chatted and cuddled into the night before turning in, exhausted. Wehia could hear the breeze and the whisper of the branches. The smoke of the fire had long dissipated. She could smell the fens this time, through the open window. Geri was already fast asleep. Wehia listened to her breathing and the soft sounds of the forge settling down for the night. She slowly drifted off to sleep…

…only to be woken up by loud noises. Fireworks? Here in the middle of the fens?

The fireworks sounded more like thunder. *Boom. Boom. Boom.* It sounded more sporadic than fireworks. There shouldn't have been fireworks…

Wehia rushed out from the bed. Bright lights rose from the fens. The lanterns. Like a mobile constellation, they ascended, flickering with urgency. Then she heard distant screams.

The encampment was under attack!

She heard running and then shouting from the women. Geri stirred, wide awake, reaching for her blades. Their door swung open. Narin stood, her eyes wide, her face stern. She held a blade made of bone.

"It's Mariad's encampment," Narin said tersely. "Soldiers have attacked them."

CHAPTER 7

WITHOUT THINKING, WEHIA grabbed Fire Heart and ran out of the room, joining the t'Nolyat women. They were all wearing light armor and bearing sharp, cream-colored bone blades. The t'Nolyat suddenly looked forbidding, a stark contrast from their fragile appearances. They reminded Wehia of the warrior women of lore. Geri ran beside her, heedless of the dawn cold. Like the t'Nolyat women, they wore light metal breastplates. Narin had opened the forge's armory. The urgent but calm methodical manner of the forge women informed Wehia that there had been previous attacks and incidents where the t'Nolyat had helped the border people.

The cold slapped Wehia's face the moment she stepped out of the manse with women. They splashed across the river, heading towards the source of the noise. There were more screams now. Sharper, infused with fear and anger. And the sound of horses whinnying. Above the women's heads, the lanterns hung like beacons. Already, some had begun their downward descent to plummet like falling stars.

Wehia could see them. Soldiers. Harassing Mariad's people with their snorting horses and weapons. They were using the border people for sport, laughing and cursing at the women who pelted them with coal and stones. Men rushed at the soldiers with sharpened staves. One of the riders toppled from his mount and was immediately set upon by a group of men and women bearing halberds. His screams were abruptly cut off. A burly soldier, his bulk unmistakable even in the pre-dawn light, was swinging about a mace. The weapon caught a few men and women, hitting their faces, crushing their limbs. Bones crunched. The victims fell like leaves.

Someone shouted, spotting the t'Nolyat women. The horses swung towards them, their hooves loud and relentless. For a moment, Wehia stared, frozen to the spot. She had never seen a regiment at full charge before. *And they* will *attack women*, she thought, repulsed by the realization. It felt abhorrent and distasteful that some men would do that. She reached for Fire Heart. Her blood was up. She wanted to fight. She was ready.

She wanted to protect the border people.

She raised Fire Heart up, settling into a defensive stance. *Stand firm, Wehia. Stand firm.* Her heart pounded. *Where is Geri? Geri! Is Geri safe?*

A soldier leaned over, his blade hitting Fire Heart's edge. The impact shook Wehia's sword arm, the tremor traveling up her elbow to her shoulder. It was sheer agony. Instant, hot tears brimmed under her eyelids. She stifled a cry. This was no ordinary swordplay. The man wanted to kill. He yelled something at her. He thought she was a boy. He jumped off his horse, still holding onto his sword. He shouted a challenge. He wanted to kill. She was a border person. She must die.

He rushed her without preamble, without the formal courtesy and grace she was used to during her training and sparring. She only had enough time to block his strike, gasping at his brutal strength. She was up against a fighting man and fighting men obviously didn't heed the conventions of swordswomen nor genteel swordplay. He was going in for the kill.

She caught glimpses of his face. Bearded, a faint scar across his right cheek. Breastplates. Dark leather. Chainmail. Grizzled temples. Was he someone's father, someone's son? He was now a monster attacking her.

Then the blade sang down again and Fire Heart flew up to meet it. Strike, parry, strike, parry. The blades rasped and shook. Wehia had never experienced such rigor, such violence before.

She was fighting for her life.

The soldier moved in, using his body as a weapon too. Wehia gasped painfully. She hadn't been trained to fight like that. She hadn't been taught to kill people, not even when it came to duels. He *had* been. Wehia smelled rancid breath and body sweat mixed with the heady odors of weapon oil and leather. Horse manure too. She tried to kick him away. Her foot struck his groin. He cursed at the pain. His body felt like a wall.

Strike, parry, strike, parry. It seemed to go on forever.

He was becoming impatient. Around them, the skirmish was almost over. The encampment was burning, torched by the regiment. The smoke was as thick as the one that had blanketed the fens weeks ago. Had the fires been started by the soldiers too? They obviously wanted the encampment dead. Gone. Existence erased.

"Why don't you just die, vermin?" the man spat viciously. He swung his blade down for the killing blow. Wehia raised Fire Heart frantically in a defensive guard, blocking the blow.

In that split second, she thought of Fire Heart's flaw…

Everything *shattered*. Wehia felt fire slice right through her right shoulder. The shock made her scream aloud. The fire continued to sear through her body like a keen blade cutting through soft butter. She could smell hot copper and a wetness was spreading down her arm. Her knees became water. She could only hold onto Fire Heart, fighting vertigo and the urge to just topple over. Wehia's hands trembled. Her right arm was becoming cold, as if she had just plunged it in ice water. Why was the blade so light? Why was it growing so dark around her? Why was she feeling so weak? She groaned and rammed the blade blindly into the man's stomach. She felt it go through flesh and hit solid bone. The soldier flinched and then jerked violently with a spasm. She yanked the blade out, half in shock, half in rage. The smell of hot copper grew heavier, more intense.

She heard Geri shouting her name. Why did her voice sound so far away? She saw blurred figures, glimpses of open mouths, horses running.

The world spun. She spun. The night sky spun.

Wehia fell and Fire Heart fell with her.

Agony roared inside Wehia like an uncontrolled forge fire. In her pain, she kicked and screamed, resisting any help. She dropped into a deep wall of darkness, regaining consciousness briefly, only to fall back into a comfortably numb black nothingness free from pain. In this void, she whirled like a star, like a glowing lantern, joining thousands of stars like her. She hung suspended before she flew down with spread crane wings woven from constellations. *"Not yet,"* the stars seemed to sing. *"Not yet."* When her feet touched the earth, she ran on all fours, sleek and fleet of foot like the ore-dogs back at home.

Wehia woke up desperately thirsty. Her entire body was tender and sore. Her eyes were gummed together by tears. She opened her eyes, suddenly afraid that she had died. Maybe she had. *"Not yet,"* the stars sang.

She was in a room with light-brown walls. It smelled of clean laundry and the faint hint of fen pine scent. Her nose remembered the hot, coppery odor. Was it blood? Was it *her* blood? Did she bleed too much? Why was she bleeding? She couldn't feel her right arm and hand. *I can't feel my right arm and hand.*

"Wehia." A figure swam into her view. It was Geri, still alive and well. Her eyes were bloodshot. Was she crying?

"Water." Wehia could only croak. Her voice was so soft! Geri disappeared briefly, only to reappear with a white ceramic cup. She helped Wehia sit up and pressed the cup gently against her lips. The water was ambrosia: sweet, cold, and clean. Wehia drank eagerly and hungrily. She was parched. Her stomach was hollow.

"Rest." Geri spoke the moment Wehia had finished the water, as if she wanted to forestall any more questions from Wehia. "You need your rest."

"Am I hurt? What happened? Did we win? Did the soldier die? Did I kill him? How come I can't feel my right arm?" Wehia wailed.

"We carried you back. We won," Geri said. "Now rest. Please."

"I can't feel my right arm! Why isn't my hand not moving?"

"You were injured. You will heal. Now, please, you need to rest, amal," Geri whispered softly. "Please, Wehia."

"Where's Fire Heart? Where is it?" Wehia glanced around frantically. Her sword was not beside her. Her heart beat painfully, just as bad as the ferocious agony she'd felt earlier. She couldn't breathe. How long ago had it been? Had it been yesterday? A few days ago?

What happened? She remembered the soldier falling over. She remembered dropping Fire Heart. Why had she dropped it? Had it broken?

Did it break?

"It's…" There was a flicker of emotion on Geri's face. The girl bit her lower lip, unable or unwilling to continue.

"Did it break? Tell me the truth!" Wehia was almost shouting now. "*Did it break?*" Tears rolled down her face. She hurt. She hurt all over. And if Fire Heart had really broken… Her world crumbled. Whatever she'd done had been for nothing.

She prayed that fervently it wasn't true.

The fracture… The fracture.

Fire Heart broke.

And she was at fault.

Geri sat down beside her, stroking her brow gently. "The truth? It broke, Wehia. It shattered. Fire Heart broke." She stopped, closing her eyes. Her brassy fringe hid her face. "I am so sorry."

Wehia sobbed this time, her heart breaking into a million pieces. She had failed. Her world had shattered. Clearly distraught by Wehia's crying, Geri gave her a strong herbal brew to soothe her wounded spirit and to make her sleep. Wehia sank under, her pain temporarily numbed and taken away by the medicine.

Despite Geri's admonishments, Wehia insisted on seeing Fire Heart once she felt strong enough to sit up without assistance. Her entire right shoulder and arm were wrapped in thick bandages. The bandages were blood-stained and cumbersome. They smelled too of herbs and cleaning solutions used by the t'Nolyat surgeon. She still could neither feel her arm nor move her fingers. The surgeon advised her to give it a week or more for the nerves to recover and heal.

Geri had also explained what happened after she and the others had saved Wehia. The regiment had fled the scene, having done what they'd been tasked to do. Mariad's encampment had been in full disarray and the leader had made the decision to move to another site. They had many wounded and dead. Saddened and angered, Mariad had vowed never to trust the City again. Narin was certain that this dawn raid might have pushed the stoic woman to the side of the more violent-minded encampment leaders. The forge mistress rued the actions of the soldiers, saying that they had caused more rifts in recent times. As a precaution, Narin had posted capable forge women as sentries to guard the manse.

Wehia's mouth went dry when Geri brought in a

cloth-wrapped bundle, cradling it carefully in her arms. Wehia felt faint. She realized she wasn't ready to look at Fire Heart. Throughout the week, Wehia had fallen into a dark spiral of self-blame and feeling like a failure. Her thoughts repeated themselves. She wallowed in them. She'd broken the sword. She was no longer a senior apprentice. She was a failure and she deserved it.

Geri had sent word out to Hadana. They had already crossed the four months' deadline. According to Geri, Wehia had been unconscious for four days. The t'Nolyat surgeon and attendant healers had worked on her injury, stemming the bleeding and stitching the wound before padding it up with herbs and bandages. Wehia burned inside out with furious shame. She didn't want to hear Hadana's reprimands or even pity. What if her mother knew? A broken blade and a daughter who was not whole anymore? Her sisters, aunts, and cousins would all laugh at her.

The t'Tolani girl placed the bundle next to Wehia before unwrapping it layer by layer. Wehia forced herself to look at it. She had only herself to blame.

What she saw broke her heart twice over.

Fire Heart's handle and cross guards were intact. It was the blade that had snapped into four distinct parts, starting from where the cross guards met the base of the blade and ending with the jagged fragment that was the tip of the sword.

And the song embedded deep within Fire Heart, the song that had inspired Wehia to create it, Fire Heart's voice, was *gone*. Snuffed out like a candle flame in the wind. Search as she could, she could no longer hear it. All she could see in her mind's eye was a heart that wept crimson blood.

"The heart of the sword broke." Wehia moaned. She felt hot tears return. She let them flow. "I tested it, Geri. I tested it many times, but it didn't break. What happened?"

"I can't say, Wehia," Geri answered, stroking Wehia's forehead. "Blades break. It happens."

"I tested the blade. The components were fine; the measures were correct. Did I not temper it well? I made the heart strong!" Wehia had to use her left hand to touch Fire Heart's handle. Touching the sword reassured and hurt her at the same time. "I stress-tested it. I sparred with the women. I heard it sing. What happened?" She knew she was repeating herself. She was falling back into the spiral again. She didn't care. In the end, it was useless. Fire Heart had cracked. Fire Heart had broken.

Fire Heart had a fracture. The thought sounded just like Hadana: wry and gently questioning.

"Would you reforge it?" Geri asked, her tone kind. "It's still Fire Heart. You made it. We are not going to hold it against you. This sort of thing happens all the time."

"I made it!" Wehia hissed. "I *made* it. I was supposed to make it strong. But it cracked. Am I not a forge woman too? But, look, it still broke. It still shattered under pressure."

"Wehia, you are delirious. You were fighting a soldier!"

"It broke, Geri. It had a fracture. It broke!"

"For the Goddess's sake, I *know* it broke. I want you to think for a moment. Would you forge it back again? You have to reforge it. Or are you going to run away because you're too ashamed to face your mistake?"

Wehia knew Geri was right. Geri was always right. Shame and failure were twisting Wehia's mind and guts. Should she tell Geri the truth?

"Can you give me some time to think? I…I'm not ready to do anything now. I just feel like a failure. I have failed everyone," Wehia said, her voice tiny. Her heart fluttered like a frightened stolati hummer chick.

Geri got off the bed. "Would you want to take Fire Heart away for a moment? I know that looking at it now gives you pain."

"No, just leave it here. I want… I want to look at it."

"Will you be all right? I'm worried for you, amal." Geri placed a gentle hand on Wehia's arm.

"I am in a lot of pain, Geri. But… I'll be fine. I'm not going to run away."

"I am going to go prepare for our trip back to the City. Rest. Sleep. Don't think too much."

Geri kissed Wehia's cheek lightly before walking out of the room. Wehia watched her leave before she turned her attention back to Fire Heart's broken pieces. Geri wasn't wrong; the sight of the shattered blade gave Wehia pain and wound her gut into tight knots. She had to face her mistake. She had to. Using her left hand, Wehia touched the four parts, mindful of the sharp edges. Her finger slowly traced back to the intricate cross guard, to the intersection that was the heart of the blade. Why had the sword broken? Had she tempered it incorrectly? Had there been a structural problem deep inside the blade she hadn't been aware of?

Only… *Had* she been unaware?

Fire Heart had had a fracture.

Fire Heart had broken.

Was she going to reforge the sword?

Wehia t'Doniyat *ef* t'Tolani.

Failure.

With a loud sigh, Wehia tore her gaze away from the mirror. The spartan room in the t'Nolyat's modest infirmary had a polished bronze mirror on the plain wall next to the medicinal cabinet. She often used it to examine her reflection.

The fingers of her right hand twitched. Pinpricks of pain crawled up and down her arm. Sensation now had come back, much to her relief. She could move her right arm. The healers cautioned her not to overstrain herself. She couldn't afford to lose both her arm and hand. So they taught her exercises to regain back mobility and tactility; she flexed her elbow, wriggled her fingers, and lifted her arm up and down.

Wehia was sure that even if she had lost the use of her limb, she could still work at the forge. There were forge women she knew who had lost their limbs due to accidents at the forges. They carried on with their work, adapting to their disabilities, and still made excellent blades. Even if she'd lost some of the vitality in her right arm, she could still use a sword. Nobody would make fun of her.

Except herself.

Her heart felt hollow. Numb.

Geri had packed their belongings neatly into cloth bags. Fire Heart was carefully and lovingly wrapped in muslin cloth. Wehia insisted she would carry it, like an infant. Hadana's cautioning words looped in her mind. Was she an unfit creator? Maybe that was why Fire Heart had fractured.

Had she caused Fire Heart to break?

"Are you ready, amal?" Geri stood at the door, an attentive shadow. She was dressed in the same t'Tolani blue robes she'd worn the day they'd arrived at the t'Nolyat holding. "They're here."

Wehia only nodded. Geri scooped the bags up and slung them on her back. Wehia had Geri strap Cold Steel on her belt. She lifted Fire Heart and cradled it in her arms. Her right shoulder pulsed with an intermittent ache. She wasn't fully healed.

The t'Nolyat women had all assembled to bid them farewell. Even the children sniffed and wiped their tears. As Wehia walked slowly towards the main door, soft hands patted her and people spoke words of encouragement. At the door stood Narin t'Nolyat, tall and regal, clad in her pale shawl and gown. She leaned close and kissed the two girls on their cheeks like an aunt would to beloved nieces.

Hadana had sent a simple blue-hued palanquin

with five forge women to serve as bodyguards and bearers. They all looked as if they were ready to fight—slung with blades, their manner grim. Like the t'Nolyat women before, they wore light armor in the color of the holding. Wehia saw the emblem of the crane embossed on their shoulder guards. Two held halberds fitted with steel crescents. Wordlessly, gently, the women helped Wehia up into the palanquin and drew the thick, velvet curtains to shield her from the outside. Inside the palanquin were comfortable cushions and blankets, in various shades of blue. Geri walked with the rest of her kinswomen.

Wehia held onto Fire Heart. Cold Steel rested beside her. The palanquin rocked as the forge women began their long walk back to the jetty. The rocking lulled Wehia into a light slumber. Geri had given her a herbal draught to steady her nerves and make her sleep through the journey.

She woke up when they reached the jetty. Geri helped her down from the palanquin, assisting her up the jetty plank. Greenish water splashed under her. Vertigo made her nauseous. Wehia saw thick black steam and the City in the distance. She was leaving the fens. She was going home. Where was home? She leaned against Geri throughout the entire voyage. The burly women stood around them like watchful sentinels, breaking their silence only to share some food and sips of fresh water from a water bottle. The two with the halberds hung close by. The bread tasted dry and bland in Wehia's mouth. She forced it down against her stomach's earnest protests.

When they finally disembarked, Wehia was sore and weak all over. She was trembling. The effects of the herbal draught had worn off. She desperately wanted water. Her head throbbed. A dismal, sharp pain stabbed at her right eye. She tried to drowse. The palanquin swayed. She could hear noises: vendors shouting about their wares, laughter, and the resonant bells of the Shrine. She smelled hints of street food, of spun sugar, toffee fruit and flour fritters deep fried and soaked in syrup. Nausea threatened to overwhelm her.

The rocking stopped. She heard women's voices.

"Welcome back, Wehia t'Doniyat *ef* t'Tolani," a familiar, husky voice said.

Hadana and senior forge woman Rika supported Wehia up the spiral staircase. The t'Tolani holding seemed to have remained unchanged. Sounds of industry emanated from the forge. The kitchen rang with laughter and chopping. It was close to early evening. Servants swept the courtyard. The stolati darted about building their tiny, cup-like nests. The fig leaves were a vivid green.

Wehia's room had been left unchanged too. Someone had aired it, allowing fresh air in. The bedsheets had been washed and changed. Folded clothing rested at the corner of her bed. The mantle had been dusted, the stolati hummer nests and other mementos cleaned.

"Rest. You had a long journey," Hadana said. She was dressed in a simple blue dress, home wear for t'Tolani women when they were not working at the forge. "We will talk later."

"My sword," Wehia blurted out.

"Not now." Hadana's reply was firm, but kind. "I will allow you to keep Fire Heart with you."

Wehia closed her eyes, biting her lip to stifle a sob. Cold Steel leaned against the wall beside her bed.

"Sleep, Wehia. We will bring a tray up for you," Rika said, her stern face softening. The two senior forge women closed the door gently.

Wehia sighed. She could hear distant partying and music. Was it already the month of the Shovel?

She still felt leaden. The herbal draught was strong. Her senses were buried under layers of wool. She was prone to drowsiness.

Wehia slept, guarded by her swords.

CHAPTER 8

THE MAN WAS *rushing towards her, his face a hateful, twisted mask. His sword was aimed towards her heart. Terrified, she raised Fire Heart up to block its downward descent.*

Everything shattered as if a mirror had broken into a million stars. Fire lanced down and through her body. She screamed and shoved Fire Heart blindly into the man's stomach...

Wehia sat up on her bed, bathed in cold sweat. Her nightshift stuck to her skin. A sharp pain radiating from her right shoulder reminded her of the injury and where she had been. For a moment, she couldn't breathe. Her heart was beating so rapidly that she thought it would soon jump out of her body. Everything hurt.

The medicinal brew had worn off, no longer dulling her pain. Geri had brought it up to her the previous night with her dinner of plain broth and a mug of watered-down sookee. Wehia ate haltingly. Her appetite was poor. She sipped the sookee, grimacing at the sweetness. Someone in the kitchen had added too much honey. Tired, she couldn't talk to Geri and took the brew instead. It was extremely bitter like burnt bark and she finished it in a few swallows. Geri approved.

It worked quickly and Wehia soon dropped into a fitful slumber filled with disturbing dreams. She kept dreaming of the soldier dying in various ways. The pain, though, was still the same, a fiery knife-like agony that cut through her very being.

She swung her feet out of the bed. Geri had fitted cream-colored socks on them. It was still an hour or so before dawn. The City was slowly stirring. Outside, soft voices and footfalls along the corridor meant that some of the t'Tolani forge women had already woken up. Wehia blinked. Only a few weeks ago, she'd heard similar sounds at another holding.

Lifting Cold Steel, Wehia stifled the sudden muscle weakness in her limbs. Her right hand could move now, her fingers curled around Cold Steel's handle. Her right arm was still stiff. Cold Steel felt heavier than usual. She attempted a Figure-Eight drill, her entire body protesting, her right shoulder smarting immediately…and she gave up halfway, dropping the sword onto the bed resignedly.

She might never use a sword to fight again.

Wehia climbed back into her sheets and curled up into a ball, feeling sorry for herself.

Later in the morning, Geri brought her to the ablution room, where Wehia bathed with the t'Tolani girl's aid. Wehia cringed when she saw the bandages on her shoulder. She hadn't gotten used to the sight. She thought the bandages were ugly. An unnatural lump or growth on her shoulder, all crinkly and smelling of dried blood and herbs.

Then, bathed and clean, Wehia was ready to go back to her room. Geri gently coaxed her to join her and the others for breakfast at the dining hall. Wehia wanted to refuse, to hide, and push Geri away. Yet she could see why Geri was doing this. She wanted Wehia to move on and put the past behind her. She wanted to show how supportive the holding was. So, against her better judgement, Wehia held Geri's hand and followed her down the staircase. Geri did not force Wehia to walk quickly. Instead, she quietly guided Wehia by avoiding all the sharp corners and urging Wehia to be careful with the steps. When she and Geri finally reached the dining hall, Wehia was red in the face, breathless. Everything seemed to spin in front of her. She had never felt so weak before!

There was a sudden hush the moment they walked in before noise resumed once more. The forge women said nothing as Geri led Wehia to the table they often shared with the other senior apprentices. One of the younger girls brought Wehia a bowl of watery grain porridge and a mug of warm sookee. Wehia stared at the grains swimming in the bowl.

"You have to eat, amal." Geri tried to coax her with some bread. Wehia found that she missed the nutty palm bread of the encampment.

She had no energy to argue back. She nibbled at the bread and ate a few mouthfuls of the porridge. It was bland. The sookee this time was less sweet and creamier. Queasiness stayed her tongue too. She hadn't eaten so much in a while. Convalescent food at the t'Nolyat holding had consisted of light broths and herbal teas.

Wehia noted that the senior apprentices were watching her. They glanced away guiltily the moment she looked them in the eye. She'd left the holding a few months back with the holding's blessing, only to return with a broken body and spirit. She suffered an intense pang of embarrassment not for using the gifts given to her by the forge women.

The way back to her room was saturated with

silence. Wehia was just glad that she didn't see Hadana or Rika around. Geri explained that Hadana was out visiting a holding in the next street with Rika accompanying her. They were there to negotiate a collaboration with the holding.

"Some lady wanted a complicated weapon, which required the two holdings to work together," Geri said, her hand soft on Wehia's arm.

Life in the City had simply continued on blissfully without a care about the fens. They were indeed worlds apart.

The man was rushing towards her, his face a hateful, twisted mask. His sword was aimed towards her heart. Terrified, she raised Fire Heart up to block its downward descent.

Everything shattered as if a mirror had broken into a million stars. Fire lanced down and through her body. She screamed and shoved Fire Heart blindly into the man's stomach…

The dream repeated for three more days. Wehia would wake up after the dream, her skin chilled, her heart beating painfully. Geri tried comforting her, taking her to the courtyard for slow walks in the early morning and helping her with the daily exercises. The t'Tolani forge women treated her with kindness and allowed her to assist them with light errands. Her energy was gradually returning. Her courage, however, remained to be found.

Hadana's silence frightened Wehia the most. Since she'd come back from the negotiations with the t'Karin, Hadana had been holed up in the forge with other commissions. The spring months would often give rise to a spate of gift-giving amongst the blood families, each trying to outdo the other with elaborate and ostentatious blades. It was also the season for marriages, as the spring weather was excellent for balls and parties. Many holdings were busy with marriage gifts. The t'Tolani forge rang with industry and the shouts of the women busy stoking the forge fires. With the continued patronage of major blood families like Lord Vess's, the holding prospered. August visitors submitted more designs to Hadana or Rika. The courtyard rang with their conversations. Deals were made, promises sealed with solemn ceremonies of food and drink.

Wehia thought nobody cared about her. Even Geri had to go help with the scabbard-making and gift-wrapping. The t'Tolani made their own wrapping cloth with a distinctive blue dye known through the City and fens as the holding's color. The apprentices carefully placed the scabbarded swords, sabers, and daggers in squares of this special cloth; they wrapped and folded the cloth into parcels before they sent them out to the blood families who'd commissioned them. The t'Doniyat had their own cloth and color too. They would be busy with the summer's commissions. Wehia cringed at the thought of seeing her mother. What would she say? Was she a failure in her mother's eyes?

So, while the forge women toiled at the forge, Wehia retreated gratefully into the study. It was a good place for her to hide. She found the book of swords on the shelf. The holding's archivist had already filed Fire Heart in, meticulously copying the designs and notes from the original draft, right down to the colors and types of metals needed to make the blade. She'd even inked down marginalia Wehia had scribbled when she'd redone the design. Wehia laughed and flipped through the rest of the book, glimpsing other weapons recorded by generations of t'Tolani archivists. She saw the Sun Blade, the Moon Sword, the Crimson Tear Saber, and the Council Blade. A myriad sword types and sub-types made by renowned forge women. All carefully maintained for the next cohort of aspirants. She wondered with some sadness why Fire Heart, now a broken and ruined sword, had warranted entry in such a wondrous book filled with legends and luminaries. But all the holdings kept records. It was only routine that Fire Heart's design had been documented with the other blades made by the t'Tolani and their kin.

She went back to Fire Heart's page, admiring the design all over and realizing with a pang how exquisite and beautiful it looked. She had worked hard on it. All those sleepless nights! The powerful rush of joy she'd felt in the forge when she'd joined the various parts of the sword together! What had happened? Where had she gone dismally wrong? Had she been too impulsive, too rash? With an angry sigh, she wiped tears away. Did Hadana think she was a failure? Was she going to have her status as senior apprentice revoked?

Was she going to go back to her holding in shame?

Wehia feared Hadana's censure when it came. If it came.

Would Wehia have the courage to reforge Fire Heart?

Wehia had given up on ever seeing or meeting Hadana. Was Hadana actually avoiding her? Wehia told herself that she was imagining things. She was restless, bored by the confinement and made anxious with repetitive, worrying thoughts.

"Where is Hadana?" she asked Geri one evening. Her stomach knotted in fear. She felt bilious and unsteady. Her shoulder was taut with pain.

"She's busy with a last-minute commission. You know how some of the lords are," Geri said. "Would you like to speak to her?"

"I think she's avoiding me," Wehia said quietly.

Geri's eyes widened. "You are imagining things. She's not avoiding you. This is a very busy period for the forge. Timing is simply not on your side."

Wehia stared at the night sky. The constellations were starting to emerge with the Anvil, most prominent with its distinctive shape. She sighed. She had been sighing a lot. Where they stood, the sounds of the streets outside were muffled. There was the throb of drumming in the distance. One of the smaller holdings was celebrating an apprentice's graduation. They had earlier sent a box of moon cookies to the t'Tolani as a gift. The t'Tolani had done the same to the other holdings when she'd made Fire Heart and her status had been elevated to senior apprentice.

"Am I such a failure that she is avoiding me?" she whispered softly.

"No, you are not a failure, amal!" Geri argued hotly, her eyes wide. They seemed to shine with unshed tears. "You are not a failure, Wehia."

"My sword broke, Geri. It should never have broken. Only a failure would have made a sword like that."

"Swords break all the time. You see it happen in the forge. The forge women simply roll their sleeves up and reforge the blades again. Fire Heart breaking wasn't your fault. You were defending yourself!"

"You never had a sword you loved so much break."

Geri shook her head. "Don't say that. You're blaming yourself far too much."

"I also killed the soldier. I killed a man, Geri. I killed a man."

"For the Goddess's sake, you were defending yourself, amal! I saw your duel. He was a brute!"

"I am a failure and a murderer," Wehia said finally.

Geri held Wehia's hand and raised it to her cheek. Geri felt warm. "You are none of those. Narin and Mariad spoke positively of you. Besides, Hadana is *not* avoiding you. She will speak to you when you're ready."

When will I be ever ready? Wehia thought.

"Geri, would you hate me if I told you that Fire Heart had a fracture?" she whispered.

The t'Tolani girl squeezed Wehia's fingers. "No."

"Fire Heart… had a tiny fracture. I hid this truth

from you. From everyone. I lied because I hated the thought of censure."

Geri hugged Wehia immediately. "Oh, Wehia. I'm glad you finally told me the truth!"

Wehia exhaled slowly, tears streaming down her face.

When Hadana's censure came, it wasn't what Wehia had expected.

She found the forge mistress alone in the forge, poring over designs and patterns strewn across her personal worktable. Hadana often worked at the far-end left-hand corner of the forge, a quiet space allocated by the forge mistress for her own use. The forge women would seek her advice there. Hadana would also observe the forge from her worktable. While the forge mistress scanned the drafts, she turned a wooden model of a quillon dagger in her hand, looking at it contemplatively as she examined the object at different angles. The forge was still warm after a day of intensely hectic activity. The marriage season was drawing to a close and orders had dropped to one or two per day. Even the parties in the City had quietened down. The entire forge breathed a sigh of relief.

Wehia had been wandering through the t'Tolani holding, wrapped in a deep, dark mood. The apprentices were out on errands for the whole day, some delivering the orders, the rest helping the forge women with purchases of new material from the steel merchants. Geri accompanied Rika to the Shrine with a basket's worth of thanksgiving trinkets; they were to be hung on the walls as gratitude for the Sword Goddess's generosity and protection.

She drifted like a forgotten wraith. Her shoulder still hurt, but not as badly as before. She could move her arm and fingers easily now. She was healing very quickly. Even the t'Tolani physician, a distant cousin of the t'Nolyat healer, checked her and was pleased by how rapidly the wound had sealed. Wehia's youth and general good health had helped boost her physical recovery. However, the physician expressed concern when she noted Wehia's despondency and suggested more time for healing.

Wehia wasn't sure why she was still drawn to the forge like a moth to an open flame. The forge had been a large part of her life. She found joy in it, holding the tools in her hands, working on her blades. The smells of the forge stirred her heart and woke something in her. Lately, it was all about Fire Heart and the forge had borne witness to its genesis and birth. Wehia was so certain she was going to lose this part of her life, that she would never, ever again touch a tool or stoke the fires of the kilns. Or make a sword.

"Come in," Hadana said. "I would like some company while I amend this woeful excuse of a design. Some people submit nonsense."

Wehia caught sight of extravagant swirls on a large, rectangular piece of parchment, an elaborate cross guard. A basket shield. No wonder Hadana had to amend the design. Impractical designs were the bane of many swordsmith holdings. Many lords and ladies often wanted working blades that looked too ornamental or decorative. They wanted to be above all fashionable.

"Have you eaten? Did you take your herbal brews?" asked Hadana.

The gentleness in the forge mistress's voice, the kindness in it, made Wehia feel worse and better at the same time. The swirling, fierce emotions tore her in half.

"Yes," was all Wehia could answer. "Yes." She couldn't articulate the mess of emotions in her head, in her heart.

"Good. I want you to heal and recover," Hadana said.

Wehia blinked. Hadana had not said anything about Fire Heart. Nor had she blamed her for it breaking. Tears started to burn under Wehia's eyelids. They were hot. She blinked again and they curved down her cheeks. "Why didn't you scold me? I broke Fire Heart. *It cracked.* I failed as an apprentice." She spoke in a low voice. The tears threatened to turn into a gushing torrent, like the River Veru breaking, like the dams at her holding too full of meltwater. All the pain, all the agony wanted to burst out from her carefully maintained façade of calm.

Hadana placed her charcoal stick down on the table carefully. She leaned back on her chair, looking at Wehia closely. Under the light of the forge, Hadana appeared older and weary. Or just tired, a forge woman's lot in life.

"I will not blame you for what happened to Fire Heart. Nor will I tell you that you have failed. You are not a failure. Swords break."

"I…"

"Things happen. Blades crack under duress. Swords break under stress. Not all will be perfect."

The relentless kindness in Hadana's voice drove Wehia to further confusion. Her tears became sobbing that came straight from her heart: regret, anger, pain, and loss. She let them pour out. She'd craved this release.

"Are you afraid that I will censure you, Wehia? Judge you because you broke a sword? Because you used it to defend yourself? Because it had cracked?"

"I want you to scold me. To reprimand me. Tell me that I'm a failure! Yell at me!" Wehia shouted, knowing that she sounded hysterical. "That I didn't listen to you, that I... failed because I believed I was right...I wanted so much to help the encampments that I forgot my sword was important. I didn't test it longer. It was all my fault!"

Her shouting echoed in the large, empty forge. It sounded like soft sobbing. Hadana's expression remained the same: calm and kind.

"Wehia." Hadana shook her head. "I only asked you to watch and protect your heart."

"I am sorry, Aunt," Wehia said brokenly. "I am sorry I am such a failure. I am sorry... because I didn't listen to you. You told me not to rush through everything... but I did."

Hadana began to chuckle, which slowly evolved to merry laughter. Wehia blinked. "The Wehia I knew would fight me and resist me. Where is she now?"

"Aunt?"

"I want her back—the Wehia who would persist and carry on, no matter what. Can you find her? I want her back. I want her fighting me. I want her resisting me, arguing with me. Consider this my censure."

Impulsively, Wehia hugged Hadana. Her shoulder immediately throbbed in protest at the sudden movement. Hadana laughed softly and placed a hand on Wehia's forehead. She stroked the girl's head tenderly. "Thank you," Wehia whispered, touched by the forge mistress's kindness and compassion. Like always, Hadana smelled warm with a hint of fragrant spice, earthy, like the best polishing oils.

"I want you to heal, find your footing, and we will then talk about reforging Fire Heart," Hadana said, touching Wehia's shoulder. "I want the Wehia with a fire heart, the girl who believes passionately. Promise me that you are that Wehia still."

"I promise." Wehia bowed. "I will be fire heart and cold steel. I will be more cold steel this time." She repeated a second time, almost like a pledge. Reminding herself.

She realized that Hadana had not questioned her about the border people nor pushed her to defend her plan. This, too, was kindness.

CHAPTER 9

SOLEMNLY, WITH A lighter heart, Wehia lifted the book of swords out from the shelf. The book was heavy in her hands, heavy with history and worth. If she listened hard enough, she thought she could hear the various songs of the blades in the book. All blades had their own songs, right down to humble kitchen knives. Wehia heard a familiar and distinct note: Fire Heart. Vivid imagery rose in her mind: running brown ore-dogs tinged with hues of flame, dancing snow-white cranes with spread wings tipped in sun fire. Interwoven with these images was a twinning pattern of heart-shaped bright-green leaves and stylized orange suns. Wehia wasn't sure where it came from. Her memories of the encampment? Had Fire Heart changed too?

Had her journey back to the fens transformed her?

Wehia swallowed hard and gently turned the pages until she found Fire Heart's record. There on the page, Fire Heart lived unbroken and unashamed. Compared to its now-shattered physical form, Fire Heart seemed to shine with its own light. Forge women would say that it was from the essence of the blade.

"I'll do it," she said finally.

Watching from the doorway, Geri heaved a sigh of relief. Wehia had changed for the better and the t'Tolani girl was clearly glad to see the change in her. Wehia's speech was now more measured, her actions mindful of others. She was less prone to rushing off on a whim. Instead, she would pause and think for a moment. It had taken a serious wounding to bring about this maturity. Geri told her she wished it weren't so, but it had happened. Life was messy like that.

"I am so glad, amal," Geri said finally, kissing Wehia on the cheek.

⊢———

Wehia lay Fire Heart out before her, gently and reverently. On the uncovered worktable, the sword's shattered form was stark and uncompromising. Joining the four parts again would be…felt…like a momentous task.

With gloved hands, she caressed the broken blade. The edges were still sharp. She could see how the sword had disintegrated. The edge had taken the impact of the blow and aggravated the hairline fracture so much so the cracks had spiderwebbed through the blade.

"I'll have to take Fire Heart apart," Wehia declared aloud to herself. Speaking the words made her feel braver, stronger. "The entire blade will be made strong. I will melt it down."

Quietly, without a further word, she began the reforging of Fire Heart. There was no fanfare, no drumming, no singing. Wehia simply rolled up her sleeves and started work.

The man was rushing towards her, his face a hateful, twisted mask. His sword was aimed towards her heart. Terrified, she raised Fire Heart up to block its downward descent.

Everything shattered as if a mirror had broken into a million stars. Fire lanced down and through her body. She screamed and shoved Fire Heart blindly into the man's stomach...

Wehia woke, her mouth parched dry. She was chilled to the bone. The nightmare was back. Perhaps it would never go away. She lay on her bed, listening to her heartbeat return back to normal. Faint white light seeped through the tiny gap under the curtain. The sun had just begun to rise. There was a slight chill in the air, promising to warm up later in the day. Late summer had arrived. Where did the time go? The voices of the vendors rang out as the merchants pushed their carts selling breakfast fritters. It was the month of the Dagger.

Wehia sat straight up. Her shoulder no longer throbbed, not even when the weather turned damp and cold.

Wehia shadow-boxed for a while before donning her work clothes for the forge. She had a blade to reforge. She pushed the dream away while it couldn't hurt or scare her. Her heart sang.

She was ready.

The tajam roared into life, fanned by hand bellows. It glowed hot.

"Ready?" Geri said, her voice muffled by her face mask.

Wehia nodded. "Yes."

She melted the broken parts of Fire Heart until they turned molten gold. The bits disintegrated into the bubbling solution, sinking, disappearing. The two girls watched the fire, keeping an eye on the heat. Wehia was glad that Geri was helping her. She would rather have Geri than any other person.

Then Wehia poured the molten solution into a mold before she allowed it to cool. When she released the bar from the container, panic gripped her. She found it hard to breathe. The image of the soldier came back.

"What if I fail?" Wehia whispered aloud, staring at the nondescript dark-grey bar.

"You will not fail," said Geri, who had remained beside her throughout the process. "Amal, stay strong. I am here."

Wehia was determined to get it right this time. She would not fail. She would not. With this in mind, she began to heat the bar once more in the furnace. The bar turned a pulsing red-yellow. When it was ready, she lifted it out gently. It was time to hammer it. She worked on it, ignoring the sweat on her brow, even pushing aside the cramp in her arm.

"I am going to hammer and heat it," Wehia said aloud. This was a skill she'd learned. A long and tedious process. She vowed not to make any mistake again. She drew the sword until it reached its desired length. Hadana and Geri nodded their approval.

"Don't give up, Wehia," Geri said.

Annealing would now begin. The sword was still soft and, hence, easy to grind. Experience had taught Wehia that it would take twenty-four hours or more for the sword to cool down. A day. She coated it in dry sand. She then took this time to rest and eat, watching the blade between her breaks.

Wehia filed the edges of the sword, using the technique she'd been taught by the forge women. The blade was slowly taking shape now. She couldn't afford to be too hasty now. Perhaps she'd heat-treated Fire Heart too quickly, allowing the crack to form. Wehia pushed the thought aside. It was in the past. She had to focus. She needed to.

Geri brought her food parcels wrapped in fragrant leaf. Juicy waxed sausages brimming with bits of sweet fat; tiny silver fish grilled to perfection; fried fritters bought from the vendors. "You still need to eat," Geri reminded her.

Wehia ate, grateful for the food. Waxed sausages meant they were in the month of the Flint.

Grinding was followed by hardening. Wehia heated the blade once more in the tajam before she quenched it in the cooling pool. A cloud of hot steam plumed and hissed. She waited patiently, watching the bubbles in the pool. Almost there. *Don't be rash. Don't be hasty. Focus.*

"It looks…" Wehia examined it after the quenching process. "No cracks. No faults," she breathed with some relief. Yet she knew the sword wasn't ready yet. She still needed to temper the sword.

She heated the sword at a lower temperature, Geri helping her with the hand bellows. She quenched it once more before repeating this process a few times, often checking the blade for any flaw, any fault.

"This is your fifth quenching! What does your heart say?" Hadana asked Wehia. She had observed the young woman from the side; concern grew in her breast. "Please don't work yourself to the bone, Wehia."

Wehia peered at the sword, seeing all the cracks, all the flaws in her mind. She shook her head. "I don't think it's ready yet."

Geri found Wehia still in the forge. It was past the evening meal. Wehia sat, hunched, beside the quenching pool. Was it the sixth or seventh time now? Geri felt a sharp pang of worry. Hadana had spoken to her in private the previous night, voicing her concern. Wehia was pushing herself too hard.

"You missed dinner," she said.

"I don't think it's ready, Geri," Wehia muttered. "Amal, I don't think *I* am ready."

"Wehia, you need to trust your instincts." Geri examined the sword. The blade looked perfect. She couldn't find anything wrong with it. Wehia's hurts seemed deeper, more entrenched. The shoulder wound had healed. The scars Wehia bore were inside.

"I don't trust them. What if I am *wrong* again?" Wehia closed her eyes. She knew there were dark rings around them.

"Listen to yourself. Listen. What are you thinking?"

"What am I thinking? I'm thinking… it's ready. But I am afraid. I'm afraid the same thing will happen again. I'm afraid, Geri. I'm afraid to fail."

"Wehia."

"I don't want to fail. I don't want to!"

Wehia buried her face into her gloved hands. The tears were coming back with a barbed ferocity she hadn't expected. Phantom pain throbbed along her shoulder.

"I know. My daggers were like that too. I was afraid to fail. I almost did."

Wehia stared up at Geri, her face tear-streaked. She recalled how hard Geri had worked on her daggers. "I didn't know that."

"I was scared. I wanted Hadana to be proud of me. I wanted…I wanted my mother to be proud of me. I wanted to be worthy of the t'Tolani name."

Geri knelt down to Wehia's level and rested her brow gently against Wehia's forehead. "I want to let you know that I believe in you. Listen to yourself. Listen to the voice inside you."

Wehia inhaled slowly. Geri was right.

She had to listen to herself.

Would she dare? Did she have the courage?

After a good night's sleep, Wehia returned back to working on Fire Heart. The blade was ready. Wehia knew it was almost done. She just had to join the hilt, guard, and pommel with it. Could she do it? Could she take the final step?

As she welded and hammered, Wehia let the images flow through her. The spread wings of the crane. The wedge-headed canine head of the ore-dog.

And interwoven through them like ivy leaves was the heart-shaped leaves of the fen's wood sorrel. She let the good memories fill her and give her strength like the sun's heat. She sang while she worked, polishing the pommel and the blade. The pommel gleamed. The edges of the blade glinted. Fire Heart looked as gorgeous as it had when it had first been forged and when she'd held it up to dedicate it to the Sword Goddess.

Wehia lifted the blade to the light, trying to seek out any imperfection. Was there a fracture? Had she just seen a blemish? Oh, Goddess, was there a small line along the edge?

Would it be still as sharp?

Would it be still as resilient?

It was her sword.

It was.

My sword.

Hadana insisted that they have a dedication ceremony for the reforged Fire Heart. The affair was more subdued than the first, but the forge mistress made the kitchen staff cook up a feast of fried fish, baked fowl, and pots of morani stew with platters of fresh bread.

The drumming was quieter but earnest, the women forming a circle around Wehia to give her their blessings.

Wehia sat in the middle of the circle, mixed emotions warring inside her. It should have felt like a victory. She should have felt happy. Yet she couldn't feel either emotion in her chest. Geri kissed her on the cheek and Wehia returned to the moment, barely smiling.

"I still have to test it," Wehia told Geri as they walked back to her room. She could still hear the drumming and singing from the hall. "Fire Heart might break again."

"You have to believe in yourself," Geri said fiercely, gripping Wehia's hand. "You have to. Fire Heart is still *your* sword."

"I know." Wehia grimaced. Her room looked messy. She hadn't had time to tidy it. Piles of clothing were on the floor. Cold Steel rested against the wall.

"You wanted to make it, remember? You were so determined to forge it. Fire Heart's yours. It's part of you."

Am I broken? Wehia thought.

"You won't believe me, but the entire forge is behind you. We want you to succeed. *I* want you to succeed."

"I know," Wehia repeated. With a sigh, she sank onto her bed, suddenly heavy and hollow with exhaustion. It was late, already past midnight. She knew that she had to sleep. To rest. So that she could test Fire Heart.

Would Fire Heart fail?

My sword.

Will not fail.

I *will not fail.*

Geri spent the night with her, curled up beside her. Wehia listened to her breathing, soothed by the rhythm. She soon slept and her dreams were of running ore-dogs.

CHAPTER 10

WEHIA SPENT TWO good eight-days testing Fire Heart, subjecting it to all the stress and strength tests. She watched the blade curve and bend, struck its edges against hard surfaces, and dueled with Hadana and the other forge women to test how it fared in combat. She even tested the sword against fresh animal haunches and green stalks soaked in water and wrapped with cloth to mimic flesh and bone. All the while, her heart was in her throat; she was terrified to see yet another hairline fracture. And Wehia had known how it felt to cut a blade through real flesh. She shuddered when she cut through the haunches. The memory of the battle haunted her still.

Geri watched all the stress and strength tests with growing worry. Why was Wehia so hesitant? Was she afraid of failure?

"Again," Wehia was yelling. "We should repeat this test again." Geri furrowed her brows.

"Fire Heart looks fine!" the girl insisted firmly. They had lined a table with summer melons bearing hard rinds. Wehia sliced them with the sword. They fell off from the table, halves cut neatly. Yet Fire Heart had held up and its edges remained without nicks.

When all the tests were completed, Wehia held Fire Heart in her hands, peering closely at the blade. Had she succeeded? Was Fire Heart now whole?

Was *she* whole?

Would it crack again? Fracture under duress?

Would it break?

Geri spoke as they cleaned the courtyard with bristle brushes. "There's a story about craftswomen from the mountains. Clans of pottery makers, I heard. They're skilled in fixing broken bowls and vases. I forget what the skill is called. But the pottery makers believe even broken things have beauty and value. It's the scars and cracks, they say, that make you strong and valuable." Testing with fruits was a messy affair, with the seeds and rinds scattered everywhere. The courtyard filled with the smell of fruits left too long under the sun.

"I am not sure if Fire Heart has much value," Wehia said.

"It's *your* sword. It *has* value."

Do I have value? As broken and wounded as I am? Wehia thought.

Despite Hadana's and Geri's reassurances that Fire Heart had passed the tests, Wehia insisted on continuing the tests for another week. She kept checking Fire Heart's blade after each test, certain she would see a fracture or a crack. Any blemish—even an oil stain—caused her heart to stop. She had become anxious and nervous. No matter how many times Geri had told her that she shouldn't be afraid of Fire Heart breaking again, Wehia couldn't stop replaying the day she had first seen the tiny fracture. It had been long ago, last year's history, but she was terrified of the same mistake.

At last, when the final test was completed, Wehia sank to her knees, exhausted of both mind and body. Fire Heart lay before her, gleaming still even after all the tests. She squinted. *Why is there a smudge? Is it a hairline fracture? What have I done wrong again?* Something heavy like an iron fist was crushing her lungs. She couldn't breathe.

Aware of her growing panic, Wehia inhaled deeply. *I am afraid,* she realized.

She lifted Fire Heart and held it against the light of the afternoon sun. It shone, the edges glistening. She could hear its song, bright in her mind. If Fire Heart was strong, so should she be. The wielder of the sword had to be worthy to hold and use it. What had Hadana said before? That the maker of the sword had to be strong too?

I have to be strong, Wehia thought, conviction surging inside her breast. She slid Fire Heart into its scabbard. She suddenly wanted a long soak in the bath. And sleep. Yes, sleep would be good.

What is strength? How do I become strong? What should I do?

She was grateful for the support she had: Geri, Hadana, and even her mother, though they hadn't spoken since her last visit home. Plus, the holdings were pretty much family. She was surrounded by family. Was this one of her strengths? She often thought she was confident and quick-witted, a proud scion from a swordsmith holding. Could she rely on her own strength too?

Did her swords give her strength? Could she be somebody even without Fire Heart or Cold Steel?

Fire Heart in her arms, Wehia walked towards the stairs.

Perhaps time would tell.

⊢———

When Wehia was finally satisfied with Fire Heart's performance, she declared the reforging and testing done. Hadana and Geri heaved a sigh of relief. By then, it was in the middle of the Flint; sausages sizzled on holding stoves and street vendor grills. The smell of cooking sausages filled the air. There was a festive mood in the City. Hadana felt it was a fitting end to the trials and tribulations Wehia had gone through. The past was the past. It was time for Wehia to move on. The forge mistress was eager to have Wehia complete her apprenticeship.

"Time to put your childish notions to rest," Hadana said firmly. "Focus on your apprenticeship."

Wehia frowned at those words. Childish notions? It wasn't childish, what she had experienced at the fens, with the t'Nolyat and Mariad's encampment.

"Aunt," she said slowly. "My *notions* are not childish."

Hadana's face bore a slight smile. "Forgive me, then. But I certainly want you to have a concrete plan next time."

"Have you heard anything from Aunt Narin?" Wehia ventured. She hadn't heard any news from the fens. Whatever had happened to the encampment?

"She has sent us her well wishes and the express hope you have recovered. The en—" Hadana lowered her voice and drew Wehia aside. It was a busy forge. "The encampment is well. No attacks since then. You do know it's still dangerous over there, right, Wehia?"

I killed a soldier, Wehia wanted to say, but she bit her tongue. "I am glad they are well," she said aloud.

Hadana nodded, evidently pleased with Wehia's response. She left Wehia alone then, citing her eagerness to supervise yet another commission. The girl stood, listening to the forge, to the chatter of the forge women and to the sounds of the tools.

I want to see the Council Sword, Wehia thought suddenly. She had caught a glimpse of it, when she'd passed by the Council Hall a year ago, when she'd been on one of her errands. It had rested on a special dais in the middle of the magnificent Council Hall. The Council allowed tourists to visit. The Council building was as important a tourist spot as the Goddess Shrine. Then a crowd of pilgrims had obscured her view and she'd had to hurry on to deliver a box of tools to a holding. For the rest of the year, she'd simply had no time to visit the Council Hall. Now was the perfect chance.

"I'll go to the Council Hall," Wehia whispered.

Geri was, not surprisingly, concerned when Wehia told her about her plan to visit the Council Hall.

"Wehia…" Geri said sternly. "You just recovered and Fire Heart has been reforged."

"I am not going to march into the assembly," Wehia said blithely.

"Why am I not convinced?" Geri rolled her eyes.

"I promise I'm not going to." Wehia grinned.

"I will join you, amal," Geri said firmly.

They decided to visit the Council Hall at week's end, on the seventh day when apprentices had free time. It would just be a touristy jaunt, a late morning's visit before they dropped by at the Shrine for blessings. Wehia informed Hadana and was happy the forge mistress granted her permission.

Wehia and Geri made sure any last-minute chores were done for the day before they headed out for their visit to the Council Hall. Sure enough, they were asked to mop the floor of the forge. They did so quickly and efficiently, having done so many times before. Then they grabbed their cloaks and some coins, glad to enjoy a free day with one another.

The sky was a lovely, marbled blue, no smoke

streaks and smog, this Flint seventh day. Wehia and Geri joined the throngs of City folk, tourists and pilgrims walking down the streets. Wehia loved the festive atmosphere, inhaling the fragrances of sizzling sausages and candied nuts wafting from the street vendors and admiring the dazzling variety of clothing. There were women from other swordsmith holdings; men and women from the fishing settlements; and groups of mountain folk, clad in ermine fur, visiting the City to pray at the Sword Goddess Shrine. Most were heading towards the Shrine; the month of the Flint was a time when people prayed for safety and prosperity during the autumn and winter months.

Pairs of mounted soldiers kept watch close to the Shrine and the domed Council Hall. Wehia skirted away from them nervously, memories of the attack still fresh in her mind. They bore the livery and insignia of a known blood family: the Jurians. Everybody recognized the swooping hawk. The Jurians' main purview was defense of Metakse. It was appropriate, then, to have them sending their soldiers to patrol the Shrine and Council Hall.

Wehia and Geri walked on, following the flow of traffic up the straight road that linked the Shrine to the Council Hall. They caught sight of the white dome; it gleamed brightly under the late-afternoon sun. Its beauty took Wehia's breath away—only for a moment—before she remembered the rift between the border people and City. The City played a part in the plight of these people!

Many tourists strode up and down the vast stairs leading to the main Hall. Two large stone felines stood guard at the bottom of the stairs, their mouths bared in snarls. With Geri beside her, Wehia carefully ascended the steps, noting how worn and smooth they were. Thousands of feet had walked the stairs for generations. They had to push past gawking tourists from blocking the entrance. The pointing tourists were admiring something...

And there it was: the broken Council Sword.

Guarded by four sentinels standing at four corners, the Council Sword rested in the middle of the Hall, glowing in a pool of sunlight. A white cloth draped on the dais as if to protect the sword from blemishes or touching less hallowed surfaces. The stern sentinels would not allow the tourists and visitors to come any closer. Wehia gasped at the sword's elegance and winced softly at the sight of the broken shards, jagged silver stark against the white marble of the dais. The Council Sword had snapped into two parts. She could see the workswomanship behind the blade. The pommel was simple but had been rendered well into the shape of a silver five-pointed star. The blade was without ornamentation, unadorned by complicated patterns like swirls, its clean lines speaking for itself. If it had indeed been made by Yin t'Idan, it was truly a superlative sword. Wehia was looking at a weapon forged by an ancestress. She felt a surge of pride. An ancestress!

"It's a faith line sword," Wehia noted. "Look at its fullers, its keen edge. Like Fire Heart."

Geri was clearly moved by the experience. Her eyes were misty. "And sundered too."

Wehia glimpsed dark smudges along the sharp edge of the sword. Dried blood? Her nose wrinkled. Why had the Council not cleaned the sword? Had it been to remind them of their own shame?

Visitors were not allowed to enter the assembly hall. A debate was in session. Two solemn guards stood at the huge, brown door. Wehia decided that it was time to leave. They still needed to visit the Shrine for blessings. It was also getting late. Apprentice free day was about to end.

"Lady Wehia," said a familiar male voice. Lord Vess walked towards them, his gait confident, a man who knew the Council Hall and power. Wehia and Geri bowed politely. "You must be Lady Geri."

Geri smiled, nodded, and bowed again demurely,

seemingly awed by his presence. Lord Vess had quickly nulled his son's betrothal with Geri, since she had been unwilling and hadn't accepted the man's advances in the first place. Vess had been furious at his son for not informing him and for trying to force Geri to marry him. Such things were illegal.

"A good afternoon to you. Visiting the Council Hall?" Lord Vess wore his ceremonial robes with a golden chain around his neck. A sword hung at his side. Wehia could see that it was the same blade he'd used to duel with her.

"Yes. We are enjoying our free day," Wehia answered, smiling. She liked Lord Vess. Liked him for his honesty and integrity. So unlike his son, Lord Marik, whom she considered deplorable.

"This is a lovely Flint week's end. I bid you two well." Lord Vess smiled, his lined face creasing even more, before bowing deeply. He soon left, meeting a cluster of well-dressed men and women who were clad similarly to him. Council members. They started talking and walked away, apparently discussing grain storage for winter. Wehia saw a white lion rampant on Vess's robes. It reminded her of…

…the brutish soldiers beating the border man…

…the same livery, the same insignia…

Lord Vess?

"Wehia!" Geri hissed, tugging at her sleeve urgently. "*Wehia!*"

"Did you see that?" Wehia's heart was beating so hard in her chest, she thought people in the Hall would hear it. Her head swam. She was afraid she was about to faint. Geri held her steady and they both walked out of the Hall, into the fresh air. They could hear the bells at the Shrine chiming.

"Yes, I did," Geri whispered.

"I don't believe it," Wehia said. "He's a good man."

Geri glanced sharply at her. "Appearances can be deceiving. Even kind people are unkind to others." She softened immediately, seeing the dejection on Wehia's face. Wehia looked as if she might cry. "Come, let's go to the Shrine. I'll treat you to honey-glazed sausages later."

"Geri…"

"We will talk about this…in private. Here's not the right place."

With a conflicted heart, Wehia was silent for the rest of the visit to town. They received their blessings at the Shrine, lit eight candles, and slotted coins into the offering box.

⊢———

"It's unfair," Wehia said hotly after they'd returned from their adventure. "Why must he be a bad person? He was nice to me. Talked to me about swords, dueling, and even the constellations in the night sky. Why?"

"He's blood," Geri said, sharing one sausage with Wehia. She looked unhappy, as if she were recalling the incident with Lord Marik. She didn't like Vess's son. The memory of seeing the white lion rampant probably had reinforced her dislike of Vess's family. "The Vesses were powerful. It was dangerous to provoke and offend them."

"What should I do? What *can* I do?" Wehia sighed wearily. Even the sausage tasted like ash. She let her half of the sausage fall back onto the plate.

"At the moment, I think you should do nothing." Geri shook her head, quickly forestalling Wehia's reply. She knew that look on Wehia's face. She had seen it many times. It warned her that Wehia's impulsivity was still there.

"What's a good way for the Council to pay attention? A petition?" Wehia went on. "I asked Rika and Tarin. They both said a petition is usually the first step for a citizen to voice their concerns."

"What do you hope to achieve by writing a petition?" Geri asked. "Reforge the Council Sword?"

"I mean, why not? It was forged by Yin herself.

Our ancestress!"

"They don't care about our lineages now. Who are you to reforge a legendary sword?"

"It's there, isn't it? It's not a figment of our imagination." *Not tucked away in an armory to gather dust and forbidden memories, erased out of existence because of fear and shame.* "Can you help me to write the petition? I know you write well."

"I can help you…but…"

"It's *my* holding's reputation at stake. My holding's name. I want it to make swords again, not kitchen knives and utensils. We had—have—an illustrious history. We made swords and were swordswomen who protected the fens. Geri, wouldn't you want that if the t'Tolani had had their reputation destroyed? To restore your holding's name?"

Seeing the light in Wehia's eyes and hearing the passion in her amal's voice, Geri nodded slowly. "You will probably need my aunt and your mother as signatories."

Mother… Wehia swallowed nervously. She hadn't thought of her mother. By asking her to sign the petition would mean telling the truth.

She buried her face in her hands. It was not going to be easy. Telling the truth would mean telling her mother everything.

CHAPTER II

WEHIA WROTE A petition with Geri standing at her shoulder giving her suggestions. "Do this," the girl would say. "Write this instead…" The Council was quite particular when it came to the submission of petitions. It must be clean parchment paper with black ink. So Wehia prepared ink and paper, rolling up her sleeves to write. She wrote neatly in clear, distinct characters.

[*The petitioner, Wehia Jirin t'Doniyat* ef *t'Tolani, wishes to reforge the Council Sword. The petitioner believes that the Sword was forged by her ancestress, Yin t'Idan, of the line of Lunes t'Ulan. She believes that the reforging would symbolize the cessation of hostility between the City and the border people. This is for the greater good and peace of the land of Metakse.*]

"Too direct?" She stared at Geri imploringly. "Too curt?"

"It's direct in a way that they will read it without too much fuss," Geri said. "What I have heard is that they dislike flowery prose."

"I hate it." Wehia sighed. "I don't like what I've written."

She worked on the draft until she was satisfied. She showed Geri the petition.

"You need my aunt to sign," Geri said after reading it for a while. "And your mother."

Wehia dreaded the idea of having her mother sign the petition. She sat crestfallen, staring at the words. She should tell her mother the truth. She really should. Why was she so hesitant?

I'm scared, she thought. And it was true. *Why am I so frightened of the truth?* It would mean that she had to tell Rohana everything.

The truth.

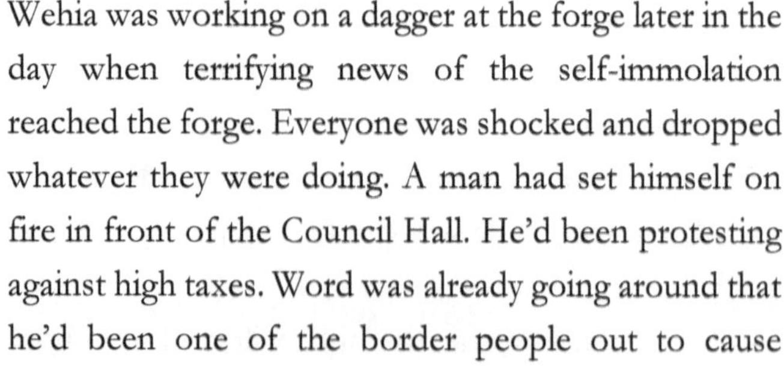

Wehia was working on a dagger at the forge later in the day when terrifying news of the self-immolation reached the forge. Everyone was shocked and dropped whatever they were doing. A man had set himself on fire in front of the Council Hall. He'd been protesting against high taxes. Word was already going around that he'd been one of the border people out to cause trouble.

Wehia felt Hadana's eyes on her. The border people again. Had the man been from one of the encampments? Had he been an outlier, someone not from the camps, and acting on his own free will?

Almost immediately, her shoulder throbbed, as if to remind her of the injury. She had to sit down, her head spinning.

"Terrible," Rika muttered. "I feel sorry for his family. This must be the third case, I reckon."

The forge women gasped. "There are others?" Tarin, one of the women, asked, her tone shocked. She was a younger woman who served as Rika's assistant.

"The previous two, I heard, were stopped by the guards before they set themselves on fire," Rika said. "Already, some people are saying it's just fabrication from the Council detractors."

"True or not," Hadana interjected, her tone heavy, weary, "this bodes ill for the Council." She exchanged a look with Rika, a look that did not go unnoticed by Wehia. What was so secretive about it? What did Hadana and Rika know? What things were they keeping from the holding?

"We were warrior women sworn to protect the fens."

"We were swordswomen sworn to uphold justice."

Had Mariad said that? Wehia couldn't remember.

Hadana clapped twice, the sound sharp and

echoing in the forge. "Get back to your tasks. We have a few commissions to complete before the cold months arrive and winter descends. Tarin, pay attention to the pommel. Lord Polos likes simple designs. Wehia, focus on the dagger. The edge has to be sharp."

Wehia shook herself and went back to sharpening the edge of the dagger.

The news of the self-immolation, shocking as it was, faded away as the forge grew busy with work. Wehia almost forgot about it, so focused she was on her tasks. Her petition was almost ready. It just needed to be signed by Hadana…and her mother.

By the end of the week, close to seventh day, more news came. Even more troubling news this time.

News of war, of a huge gathering of encampments moving their way towards the City of Swords.

The City was on edge. Anxious, the blood families stationed their soldier regiments at strategic points of the large city. Some stood guard at the mouth of the river leading up to the City. Many were sent to patrol the edge between farm and marshland, even though they knew it was hard to cross the swampy area. Wehia had chosen not to cross it two years ago before she'd become an apprentice under Hadana. She now hoped the marshland proved a challenging buffer protecting the City from the border people's wrath.

For a week, the women at the forge could hear the clatter of armored soldiers' feet and the rumble of thundering hooves. Wehia awaited with bated breath any piece of news from outside. The forge women all listened very carefully for information. The signal fires were lit. Yet the forge mistresses chose not to light the flame red, for it was the color of war. Hadana warned the news might just be hearsay and instructed the women in charge of the signal fire to stay their hand. It was pointless and harmful to spread rumors, especially during this fraught time.

"The border people haven't declared war for a long time," said one of the forge women worriedly. "Why now?"

"Perhaps they're tired of ill treatment," Wehia said, but she realized she should have kept her mouth shut. The forge women all stared at her, some reacting with their mouths in shock, some with their eyes bright in anger.

"The treaties kept them content for a while," Hadana said quietly. She had walked in, unnoticed by the forge. They were taking a break from their tasks. The furnaces still roared, watched closely by the apprentices. Hadana's hard eyes rested on Wehia. "Yet now they demand more land."

"It's their land too," Geri murmured.

"What did you say, Niece?" Hadana glared sharply at the girl.

Geri shook her head. "Just woolgathering, Aunt. Nothing more." She stirred the red coals in the furnace with a fire shovel and seemed content to watch the glowing motes drift. Hadana frowned.

There was no more discussion of war and border people. An ominous cloud hung over the forge, full of unspoken words and controlled emotions. Wehia excused herself from the forge. Her shoulder throbbed. It often did these days when she was anxious.

She found solace in the courtyard. The hummers' nests were empty now, the fig vines bare. The forge women had salvaged the prettier nests for gifts and mementos. Wehia heard the industry of the forge and the laughter of the servant women as they went about with their tasks. She hugged herself. It was getting chilly.

A soft knocking shook her out of her reverie. It was a kin code, a very familiar one that she'd known from a young age, in her bones. The distinct notes, the *thum-thum-thum* with an emphatic rhythm in between like heartbeats. With shaking legs, she headed towards the door. It was the same door from which she'd entered when she'd sought apprenticeship. The knocking grew louder, more urgent.

"Who is it?" Wehia had to ask. Must have been someone playing tricks. Must have been her ears hearing imaginary kincodes. *The t'Doniyat kincode.* What if something had truly happened to her holding? Had her holding been attacked?

A voice answered, sending both joy and coldness down her spine. "It's me, Lady Rohana t'Doniyat. I seek shelter and sanctuary."

Her hands trembling, Wehia unlocked the door. A figure stood before her, boots dusty with travel, hood drawn over her head. The figure inhaled, as if surprised to see her.

"Hello, Mother," Wehia said with a steady voice. Her heart, though, wanted to flee.

⊢——

"Would you like some more tea?"

Hadana fussed over Rohana like a clucky hen, pouring hot fen tea into her cup or plying more food onto her plate, which she left untouched. Hadana had obviously been caught off-guard by Rohana's appearance; the latter had shown up unannounced, not even with notice sent via a foot messenger. What was more puzzling was that Rohana had traveled alone without a forge woman as bodyguard or assistant.

Wehia kept her mouth shut. Inwardly, she was terrified and relieved all at the same time. Why was her mother here? Why had she come alone? Why had she left the holding? Was the holding safe? Rohana smiled and didn't say much, declining offers of food from Hadana and Rika, who looked increasingly perturbed, her forehead furrowed.

Hadana broke the silence. "What brings you to our holding, August Cousin?" Direct folk the swordsmith holdings were, direct was her speech. She had cut to the chase.

Rohana placed the cup of tea on the table. They all sat in the hall. The forge had paused their work; the women lined the corridors to greet their kinswoman, who was forge mistress and owner of a holding. Wehia stood beside her mother. She was surprised to see a sword strapped at Rohana's right side.

"I am here to see my daughter," Rohana said, her tone mild. "She must be progressing well in her apprenticeship. Senior apprentice now, I see. And she did make her sword. I am proud of her."

Wehia clenched her hands, touched but yet made more uncomfortable by the uncommon praise. Her mother doled her praise sparingly and only when she saw fit.

"Mother…" Wehia said.

"Hush, I will speak with you later." Rohana lifted her hand imperiously. "Now I need to speak my mind."

Hadana stiffened immediately, as did the rest of the women and girls gathered to welcome their kinswoman.

"What has happened, Cousin? What brings you here?" Hadana's voice could freeze water. "What is wrong?"

"War," Rohana said simply.

"War." Hadana nodded. The women glanced at one another. Fear, a cold wind, filled the hall. A few women drew closer to each other.

"I must speak with you privately, Cousin. Then I will talk to my daughter," the t'Doniyat forge mistress said, standing up gracefully. "We cannot tarry any longer. Metakse needs our help."

Hadana and Rohana spoke for a long time in the study. They had locked the door for privacy. Rika had instructed the women to go back to their work. Wehia hung around closely to the study until the senior forge woman curtly told her that molten solutions were not going to melt themselves. By then, it was close to late evening. When the two forge mistresses finally emerged from the study, it was already past dinnertime. The kitchen women had delivered food and drink to the room earlier.

Wehia caught a glimpse of Rohana's face when she walked slowly beside Hadana to the forge. It looked drawn. Weary. Hadana's too looked just as exhausted. Pale and gaunt, as if she had just heard terrible news. They were still talking in soft tones. What were they discussing? War? What had Rohana meant by *"Metakse needs us"*?

"Mother," Wehia called out. "Mother."

Rohana turned, her hard expression softening. "I will speak to you next morning. Sleep. The night is late."

"What's wrong, Mother? Is our holding in danger? Has war threatened the fens?"

Hadana looked stricken, so odd and different from

the usually stoic t'Tolani forge mistress. Had she been crying? Her eyes were red, her lips trembling.

"I did say *war*, didn't I?" Rohana said, her words frost-cold. "Now go sleep."

Wehia opened her mouth and closed it. Geri pulled her away, gently, kindly. Her sleep that night was restless. Her shoulder throbbed.

CHAPTER 12

WEHIA FOUND ROHANA out walking alone close to the kitchen. It was Rohana's habit: to wake early, before the rest of the holding was up. Her mother would pace around the holding so that she could make plans for the day and sort decisions out for the forge. This early, the t'Tolani holding was cold. Heat was only for the toilets and bathrooms. Even the kitchen fires were quiet.

Rohana had a thick woven shawl wrapped around her firm shoulders. Wehia recognized it: it was Rohana's favorite. Warm browns and oranges, woven from sheep raised by their holding's farm. Her hair, so like Wehia's, had streaks of white now. Her mother looked pensive, rubbing her hands while she walked slowly. She must have paced around the holding, walking past the kitchen, the forge, and the hall.

Wehia couldn't sleep the night before. Anxiety had woken her a few times. She'd stared at the ceiling, hearing her heart beat loudly in the silence. When dawn had come, Wehia had been glad to wake up and walk off the nervous energy.

"Mother," Wehia said. Rohana paused and turned to look at her. For a moment, Rohana looked as if she couldn't recognize her. Then she blinked and a ghost of a smile appeared on her face.

"You're up early," the older woman said. Her expression softened. "I apologize for my harsh words last night. Things are not well and I have let my fear seep through."

"Things are not well?" Wehia whispered. Cold fear gripped her throat. She couldn't breathe. It *was* her holding, then.

"The border people are hankering for war," Rohana said with an air of finality. "The news you hear is real. I have seen them mustering their forces near our holding. I don't know what to do. I came here to seek help. Your aunts stayed to protect the manse."

"No, the border people are peaceful…" Wehia muttered, shaking her head.

Rohana stared hard at her daughter. "How do *you* know?"

The truth. Now or never.

And Fire Heart. I must tell her about Fire Heart.

"Mother, I need to tell you something."

"Are you hiding something from me? Have you been lazy during your apprenticeship? Hadana has spoken highly of you. She says you are an exceptional student." Rohana stared at Wehia sharply.

"No, I'm not. Fire Heart shattered and I reforged it. And I didn't tell you this, but I visited the t'Nolyat and saw everything. The border people have two factions: some are peaceful, some are hungry for war. I…"

Rohana's face blanched, just like Hadana's. "And you didn't tell me?" The single plaintive question tore at Wehia's heart.

"I… I was afraid you might scold me."

"I would *still* scold you. I *am* scolding you! That's extremely dangerous, traveling alone to fen lands… And without telling me at all!"

"I wasn't alone. Geri was with me." She swallowed, but her mother was still waiting for her to say more. "I was too ashamed to tell you. Fire Heart…Fire Heart had a fracture. It broke. I got…got injured."

Rohana closed her eyes. "Oh, Wehia…"

"But the t'Nolyat nursed me back. They—"

"They did what they could. Ah, all the secrecy…I knew this day would come, anyway."

Wehia blinked. "I'm sorry?"

"You're an intelligent child. Impulsive and

headstrong. You didn't forget about the child you saw next to the river. And I just knew you wanted answers."

So, Rohana had been hiding things from her too. Wehia almost smiled at the irony. So much for swordsmith folk being direct. They kept secrets.

"I'm afraid I've become a failure to you," Wehia continued, breathing deeply. "I—"

"You are never a failure to me, Wehia." Rohana placed a gentle hand on Wehia's face. "Never. You never gave up. That's our bloodline. We're tough. We never give up."

"Mother…"

"You have probably heard the truth from Lady Narin. I have…I have tried hiding this from you from the moment you were born. Then you found the sword in the armory. It was hidden for a reason. Our holding was shamed for it and we were ashamed. But the truth would emerge eventually. And it did."

"I am not ashamed, Mother. We were…are…a swordmaking holding. We will become a swordmaking holding again." Wehia's heart soared. It was indeed Lady Shana's sword! Cold Steel was indeed Clarity.

Rohana laughed. It was a merry laugh. Wehia blinked, surprised. "I just knew you would say this too," Rohana said. "You must have heard the stories about us being swordswomen who protected the fen.

We did. A long time ago, when the demarcation between City and fen was not as stark. The fen people remembered the swordsmith holdings not just as blade-makers, but swordswomen too. We protected as the Sword Goddess has protected us for generations. Lady Shana did what she knew and thought best. She defended and fought for the border people against the arrogant blood."

"We were the swordswomen of old?" Wehia gasped. So it was true. Right from her mother's lips. Her heart pounded. The swordsmith clans *had* a heritage. They were the warrior women of the stories. The protectors. The guardians.

"Yes," Rohana said. "Perhaps I shouldn't have hidden the truth from you. I did so, because I wanted to protect you from harm. I was deeply ashamed of our holding's past, as were the forge mistresses before me. Maybe we were not made of stronger stuff. So I lied and I hated it. The border people were like us. Diverse, passionate, problematic. Forced to drift along the borders like ghosts. In a way, I was part of the problem. I demonized the border people, made them worse than they ever were: people who just wanted their own land, their freedom."

Rohana ceased smiling and rested on one of the chairs in the hall, suddenly looking older than she was.

"I didn't like the fictions concocted by the Council. And now they—the border folk—are angry and rightly so."

"Now there is war," Wehia said. "War that will affect City and the fens."

"Metakse needs us. Needs the swordsmith holdings to return to their rightful place denied by the blood families. Needs the swordswomen to uphold their Goddess-blessed vows."

"Would…Would reforging the Council Sword work, then?" Wehia asked.

"Ah, the Council Sword."

"I wrote a petition for it. Now I need signatories."

"I knew you would do just that too." Rohana began laughing again. "The Council leans too much on useless debate and counsel, perfect for the hawks to delay action. The stranglehold some of the families have on the holding…"

"Lord Vess…"

"Yes, him. He's one of the most vocal members eager to suppress the border people. His regiments wreak havoc in the fens."

"But he was so nice to me."

"Being nice on occasion doesn't mean he doesn't possess a hideous heart, daughter."

"He didn't defend Marik, his son. I thought he was

a good man."

"Again, being nice on occasion doesn't mean he has a good heart," Rohana held Wehia's hands. Her palms were warm. "You have grown so mature now. I am proud and pleased."

"Uh, thank you, Mother." Wehia blushed and was glad for the praise. This time, she felt her mother's approval and love.

"I'm not sure if reforging the Council Sword would work." Rohana's next words bore a note of caution. "It was broken for a reason. Yin shattered it because we didn't protect the people we'd vowed to protect. She was disappointed with all the clans and blood families alike then. We all know petitions are just words to fluff up some bureaucrat's file and lists of achievements."

"Will you sign it, though?"

Rohana nodded. "I will. Perhaps some of the old ones in the assembly still remember the swordswomen of the holdings."

Hadana and Rohana both signed the petition. Their signatures were beautiful, elaborate with the cursive writing making them elegant. Geri and Wehia checked the petition thoroughly before they sealed it with wax dyed a deep blue, the color of the t'Tolani holding. Despite their elders' warning about dangerous times, they decided to deliver the petition by hand and in person.

Rohana was right. War was coming. The City was battering down, preparing. Regiments of soldiers were everywhere, bearing halberds, spears, and swords. Most of the citizens stayed indoors, except for the truly devoted pilgrims who still visited the Shrine. Wehia noted even the street vendors were not out selling their food and wares. She and Geri walked briskly to the Council Hall, aware of the heightened security. Sentinels watched the girls walk past with steely eyes. Horses in armor stamped their hooves and worked their bits, as if eager for war to start. They no doubt felt their riders' anger and excitement.

There was something in the air, something Wehia had never felt when she'd first stepped foot into the City. Fear. It was there in the absence of the usual throngs of people. It had crept in with the shuttering of windows and bolting of doors. It danced in the cold wind. It growled in the hoofbeats of trotting horses. It whined in the form of baby cries quickly hushed by their mothers.

"They're everywhere," Geri whispered. "Lady Rohana is right. War is indeed coming."

"Let's get this over with," Wehia said, unnerved by the soldiers. They reminded her of the brutish soldiers raiding the encampment.

She and Geri clambered up the stairs, found the petition box, and slipped the sealed petition through the slot. The petition had a glass window. It was almost full. It looked as if it hadn't been opened for a while.

"They probably won't read it. But at least we tried." Wehia sighed with relief at the task done. She wanted to *run* back to the holding. She was *that* frightened.

The two girls made their way back, retracing their steps back to the holding. They walked through the narrower walkways and passages, skirting the refuse and darker alleys. A few beggars lined the walls, raising their hands up as if for alms. Something caught Wehia's eye. The vagabonds were all wearing the sunburst.

She thought of the sunburst, a gift from Narin, tucked under her pillow. Who was behind this? She didn't think it was Mariad's encampment. Were the two other leaders instigating this?

When they got back to the holding, Geri bolted the main door. Wehia felt immediately safer.

"Is it done?" Rohana asked. She had spent the entire day at the forge with Hadana.

Wehia nodded quietly.

"Now, we can only wait and pray," Rohana said.

CHAPTER 13

ROHANA INSISTED SHE had to head back to the t'Doniyat holding. Hadana persuaded her to stay a while longer since it was still unsafe to travel. The t'Doniyat forge mistress agreed to prolong her stay until the end of the week. It was already turning very cold, well into the month of the Knife. Huge snowflakes were beginning to fall, coating the ledges and the streets with a layer of white. The women were all glad for the warmth provided by the heaters.

"Would they wage war during winter?"

Wehia looked at Rohana, who was warming herself at the fireplace. The kitchen women had brewed hot sookee, a welcome beverage when it was really cold. Wehia sipped her sweet beverage and stared at her mother. She remembered Mariad talking about the encampments wanting to wage war during the winter months. Shuddering, Wehia shunted out that particular thought. It might become true.

"They would," Hadana said grimly. "Attack the City when it is vulnerable."

"We're caught in a dilemma," Rohana said. "We're supposed to help the border people."

"That was a long time ago, Cousin."

"Our oath was and still is binding. We swore to the Sword Goddess. We have to uphold our promise."

Hadana looked grimmer, pressing her lips into a thin line. "I guess you have come to terms with your holding's shame."

"For a long time, I carried it like an open wound. It's time I acknowledge it and move on. Wehia found Clarity, Lady Shani's sword. We cannot hide any longer."

"Brave words coming from you, Cousin."

"We are all kin. We all carry Lunes' blood."

"I don't suppose we march up to the Council Hall and demand they return our rights back." Hadana gave Rohana an incredulous look, shaking her head.

"No, we don't. There's more to this war, Cousin. The winds have smoke in them."

"What does Narin say about this?"

"You know what she will say, Cousin. We are kin. We fight together."

Hadana nodded. Wehia was surprised she didn't argue back. Hadana and her mother had known what they must do all along.

It was a blisteringly cold morning when news came of the attempted assassination. One of the major blood family lords had almost been murdered by an unknown assassin who had managed to slip past the guards at his mansion. The news caused a bit of a furor in the t'Tolani household. Rohana only said cryptically, "It has started." The t'Doniyat forge mistress left her words hanging, making Wehia more perturbed.

By now, the year had moved into the month of the Saber. Unable to return to the holding because of the heavy snowstorms, Rohana was forced to stay a while more. All the holdings were on lockdown. Nobody wanted to venture out. It was cold and the threat of war was still hanging in the air.

"The Council is now in session," Rika said. "Out of season. Just convened this morning. I heard from one of the street vendors when I was giving out bread to the beggars.

"They also said a huge encampment is now moving towards the City. Not across the river."

Rohana and Wehia breathed in unison. "The marshes!"

"They're going to risk a freezing-cold crossing?" Hadana lifted an eyebrow. "Daring but foolish."

"And now the assassination!" Rohana exclaimed, her face hardening. "They're gambling, Cousin. Gambling with high stakes."

Wehia and Geri excused themselves from the discussion, which was beginning to heat up. The forge women had strong opinions and were almost argumentative at times. Wehia found it wise not to linger further.

Instead, she found a space in the holding, close to the courtyard, to practice her sword drills, first with Fire Heart and then with Cold Steel. She was glad to be moving, to feel her body flow with the motions. Even in the cold, she felt warm and alive. The swords sang with her and her body sang back. It was as if Lady Shani was with her. Geri joined her with her twin daggers. The two girls practiced in silence, letting their movements form a language of its own. They danced around each other, watching each other's space, flowing with it.

Wehia disliked the feeling of stagnation gripping the holding now. She didn't like to be static. She wanted to move, to run…to do something. The City was in the midst of winter and war.

In the distance, horns blew and the Shrine's bells began to ring. The sound was so sudden, so odd, that Wehia and Geri paused their drills to listen. The rest of the holding came to join them, listening to the bells and horns intently. Rohana frowned. Hadana stared worriedly at her cousin, then at her forge women. Her roving gaze rested finally on Geri.

Then they heard it: the distinct *boom, boom, boom* of fireworks…

Only these were not fireworks. It was not the season for fireworks or firecrackers.

"You heard that?" Hadana asked.

Rohana nodded once. "Yes."

A few buildings in the main center of the City had caught fire and exploded. That was the sound of thunder they'd heard earlier. The City's firefighting teams struggled to put the fires out, difficult in the chill of winter. The buildings had belonged to small businesses selling grain and dry goods.

Now the soldiers were all stationed around the City, ready for war. The swordsmith holdings lit their signal fires, preparing themselves. They had not experienced war for generations. Metakse had enjoyed peace. The prospect of war was frightening. Yet the women took out armor and weapons from the armory without complaint and cleaned them with oil and dry cloth. Rika told Wehia that all the holdings were doing the same. Wehia ascended up the tower and saw indeed that the color of the signal fire was red. *Danger.* The women were preparing for war.

The t'Tolani armory contained swords and halberds. Wehia had never seen such diversity of types and shapes. It felt as if the holding had taken all of them out. The weapons oiled and cleaned, the women began to drill with them, watched over by Rika, who acted as drill master. She rapped out sharp instructions as the women brandished their swords and halberds, their booted feet thumping a rhythm. There was no fear in the women's movements, no hesitation.

Perturbed and anxious, Wehia went back to her room. She opened the window, desperate for some fresh air. Every place felt so stifling of late. Some distance away, the shouts of the women rang out in the courtyard as they practiced their drills.

The City smelled of snow and wood fire. Faint columns of smoke drifted from the site of the explosions. The Shrine's bells chimed. Lights flickered as households across the City prepared for the night.

Against the fading daylight, they looked like a constellation of pink, pulsating stars. They floated, drifting with the wind.

Wehia recognized what these stars were.

Wish lanterns.

CHAPTER 14

"THEY'RE ATTACKING!"

The shout came from one of the forge women serving as sentry and signal-fire guardian. Hadana raised a hand to calm the women and apprentices who had grabbed their weapons. Wehia held onto Fire Heart, Geri her daggers. Throughout the entire week, they had waited nervously. Word had come from the sentinels who'd patrolled the border between City and fen. The encampment had begun crossing the cold, swampy marshes, heedless of the temperature. It had been a small group, which raised the fear of a larger horde moving behind them or somewhere the City soldiers could not see.

It was the dead of winter, when the snow fell thick and the wind was harsh. Rohana was right: the border people were gambling with high stakes. *For what purpose and with whose lives?* Wehia thought glumly. She knew for sure it wasn't Mariad's encampment nor the encampments that fought for peace. Corwin's and Falia's? Why now? Catch the City by surprise? By throwing innocent lives into the…Wehia was not sure what to call it anymore. Rift? Conflict? Dispute? *Why must people fight?*

"The City guards are shooting back with arrows," the report continued as the woman watched from her vantage point. "There are…There are pike-men. They have…ladders! Someone's been shot! Oh, oh, ooooh!"

Rohana watched grimly, her hand holding her sword. Wehia had seen it before. Her mother used it during sword practice. She had sparred with Rohana before. Her mother was a more-than-competent swordswoman, comparable to her sword mistress.

The woman persisted in her observation. "They… They're in." It must have been a horrendous sight. She kept pausing, as if she hated what she saw. "There's… No…There's another group coming in close to the docks!"

"So, they've snuck in using the river," Rohana said, shaking her head. "Anger must have forced their hand. Anger and desperation. We have failed in our duty."

"We have failed in our duty for a long time," Hadana said drily. "The word of the swordswomen died the moment we lost the fight with the blood families."

"We are not going to let this fade again. Look at all these young women. They carry our hopes and dreams. They're the ones who will continue to uphold the vow, Cousin. Never forget this."

Rohana stared back at Hadana steadily. Wehia and Geri held their breath, fearing another argument. Hadana grinned. Tension fizzled out.

"The rate we're going," Geri whispered *sotto voce*, "we might end up breaking up *their* fight instead."

Wehia stifled a giggle. "They are Flint people. Dour, but with fiery tempers."

"At least they were not born in the month of the Dagger." Geri laughed. "Shh, there are more words coming from the watcher."

"The signal fires are lit. Arm. Gather. Guard!" the watchwoman called out.

"That's our sign to arm ourselves," Hadana said, her eyes shining. "Don your armor, Cousins and Apprentices. Prepare yourselves. Now we march to meet our kin and friends. We don our colors and gird our hearts. War is upon us."

⊣———

The smell of burning wood and smoke greeted Wehia the moment she stepped foot out into the cold. She'd been given armor plating and shoulder guards. They weighed heavily and felt cumbersome. Her arms and wrists bore leather braces. Cold Steel was strapped at her back. The women organized themselves into two orderly lines, led by Hadana and Rohana, since they were forge mistresses. The apprentices formed the back-guard. The armor was blue, the blue of the t'Tolani. Even Rohana wore blue. All of them wore helmets. A skeleton guard, formed by the kitchen and washing women, would remain behind in the holding. They had fortified the holding door with sturdy, wooden planks. They'd even set a barricade around the holding.

Wehia was not surprised that other regiments of women warriors joined them as they proceeded towards the center of the City. They had all worn their colors proudly. They too wore armor. Wehia noticed the armor worn by the swordsmith holdings was more elegant and streamlined, made to protect the vulnerable parts of the body and yet beautiful in craftswomanship.

There were weapons Wehia had never seen before. But most were swords and sharp blades. Some of the women carried morning stars and maces.

"Uncommon," Rika said after watching Wehia's startled reaction. "But some holdings still make them for the families who like close brawling. Barbaric and unnecessary, but to each their own."

The regiments met other regiments coming from all directions of the City. Every holding could only spare twenty or less. The sun shone on their helmets and armor. As the women marched down the Shrine road to the Council Hall, people gathered to watch them. Some stood by their open windows. It was cold, yet Wehia felt warm, as if the atmosphere had inflamed her very heart. Almost immediately, her shoulder throbbed. She remembered how bad fighting was. It should not have been considered a glorious thing.

We fight for the people we love and want to protect. We fight for the beliefs that keep us alive.

Those thoughts came unbidden in her mind.

For whom were the soldiers fighting, then? For themselves? For their manhood? For their families somewhere in the City?

Why must fighting for our rights mean we end up fighting and killing others?

The women formed a guard around the Council Hall building. Another detachment guarded the Shrine. As Hadana and Rohana led the t'Tolani regiment towards the Council Hall, there was—very faint—

shouting and screaming. There were flaming arrows in the sky. Wish lanterns floated. Smoke was very, very thick. Wehia's breath was hot within the confines of her helmet.

"Lady Hadana." Lord Vess stood in full armor this time. He was accompanied by the Council members in similar garb on the steps of the Council Hall. Wehia's heart clenched. She loathed him for his duplicity. "And Lady Rohana. I thought I'd recognized you by your sword type."

Rohana sketched a slight bow of her head. Vess caught that invisible cue and laughed. "Let's put aside our disagreements, forge mistresses. We have a war to fight and a City to protect."

The forge women didn't rise to his bait. Instead, they bunched together, forming a phalanx of weapons.

"Aye, there's a war to fight and a City to protect." Hadana had spoken up this time. Her voice rang clear in the still air, broken only by the shouting. "We now invoke our right and vow to protect the City."

"That's an ancient vow," Lord Vess said.

Hadana cut him off. "We have not forgotten it. We have remained silent for too long."

"Lady Hadana, there are other ways." The man's voice softened and for a moment, Wehia was taken back to the night at the docks. So long ago. They'd talked about stars and sword styles. She had thought him fatherly, a man to whom she could talk without fear. That had all been a lie, hadn't it?

"The City has long since brutalized and soured the trust between City and border," Hadana said, her eyes cold. "They wanted war because they wanted redress. The treaties didn't work, as you must have already surmised."

"I read your petition." Lord Vess seemed unperturbed. "Lady Wehia, you made good and strong points. But you should understand—"

"Understand what? That the blood families are more important than the lives of dirty border people?" Rohana said then. "And what? Revoke our right and cancel our patronage?"

"Strong words from a disgraced holding," one of the Council members said snidely. The speaker was a sturdy woman in thick, white fur.

"Hold your tongue, Lady Bartolli," Vess hissed dangerously.

"Is this really the right time to argue over old spilled blood?" Hadana asked. "I hear the border people approaching."

⊢——

An arrow embedded itself right in front of Wehia's feet. She stared at it as if it were a poisoned weapon. Then a group of men in misshapen armor rushed up, led by a tall man wearing armor that had obviously been salvaged and hobbled together, his battered sword dripping with blood. The droplets formed a line of crimson dots on the snow. His face was masked by the dragon-shaped helmet. Wehia thought he felt…familiar.

"You promised," the figure said from behind the helmet. "You promised us gold if we breached the barricades."

That voice.

That voice.

Geri stiffened. Her gloved hands grabbed onto her daggers. She knew it, too. "That voice…"

Vex.

Mariad's son.

He had betrayed his people. He'd become a traitor. For gold.

"You promised, Lord Vess," the man continued, strutting up as if he belonged. How many people had he killed? Betrayed? Did his mother know? Did Mariad know he had turned traitor?

For gold.

"Wehia…" Geri whispered.

"I know…This feels so wrong," Wehia said.

Then Vex made a gurgling sound and keeled over, clutching his midriff. An arrow stuck out of it. There was a lot of blood. Wehia's head swam. The soldiers were shouting, shouting, shouting.

Almost retching, Wehia lifted her head to see Lord Vess lowering the crossbow.

"You have blood on your hands," Hadana said, almost coolly, very calmly. Her words could freeze water. "I have misjudged you, my lord. I thought you were a honorable man. But you're not afraid to shed the blood of others. Like father, like son. The blood runs like poison in your veins."

Wehia looked at the fatally wounded man gasping for air. His men had retreated, their courage suddenly gone. They hung about like lean feral dogs, afraid to move forward and yet still wild enough to snarl and bark out their threats.

"Please rescind your patronage," Hadana said. "The t'Tolani will voluntarily go into poverty."

"Cousin, we will protect you," Rohana said and her voice was joined by the rest of the gathered forge mistresses.

Vess's soldiers had appeared, bearing lethal-looking halberds. They looked very similar to the men who had razed Mariad's encampment.

The forge women quickly formed around Hadana, Rohana, and the forge mistresses. Wehia had heard about such tactics. She had read about them in books. Now she was seeing tactics and theory becoming reality. The women formed circles, protecting the vulnerable center, where the leaders stood. Their swords, halberds, and pikes bristled.

Wehia felt a surge of fierce pride to be standing with such brave women. Indeed, they were warrior women and strong kin.

"Stand firm," Rika said through clenched teeth. "Keep your eyes open."

The t'Tolani women nodded.

The soldiers approached menacingly. Their intent was clear: to kill.

"How the City has fallen in regard," Hadana said sadly. "When its men are quick to kill for coin."

Lord Vess's face darkened. "We have no choice."

"'No choice'? The blood families always have choices because of your power."

"Lady Hadana, you stand on dangerous grounds."

"Really? Would the Council sword suddenly appear and kill me where I stand? It would only kill those who are unworthy." Hadana's tone was haughty, goading the blood family lord.

"Of course not. It's shattered. Broken. I wonder

why."

One of the soldiers rushed forward but was cut down by a t'Haniff woman wielding a halberd. The Council members tittered in fear as the soldier toppled over.

"We can continue doing this for days." Rohana sighed. "So much bloodshed."

Now or never, Wehia thought.

"We will decide victory through a duel," she called out.

"Ah, Lady Wehia, always brave and honorable," Lord Vess said.

Rohana nodded, giving Wehia tacit and silent approval.

"If I win," Wehia said, drawing Cold Steel deftly, "we will abolish the ruling that made my holding a knife-making holding and reinstate it as a sword-making clan with all its powers. And if I win, abolish all the rulings that make the border people landless and give their land back. And as a sign of this victory, I will reforge the Council Sword. Also if I win, the blood families will no longer have full rein of the Council. The swordsmith holdings will hold seats because our voices matter too."

"Witnessed and heard!" the women shouted.

"And if you lose?" Lord Vess said with a hint of

malice and doubt in his voice.

"The hatred continues," Wehia said heavily. "And the pain continues. But if *you* lose, we will let you go with your dignity intact, only that the forges will not seek your patronage anymore. Your family will be shunned. "

Wehia would not lose this time, this fight. If she needed all her strength, it was now. Her holding was a clan of warrior women, protector of the border people. In her, the clarity of Cold Steel and the flame of Fire Heart pulsed.

Geri nodded, giving her the strength she needed. "I believe in you," the girl mouthed.

CHAPTER 15

THE WOMEN FORMED a large circle, a physical boundary, around the duelists. Lord Vess stepped forward, massaging his neck and flexing his wrists before dropping easily into a guard.

Geri kissed Wehia on the cheek before she entered the ring. She had placed Fire Heart in the arms of Rohana. With Cold Steel in her hands, Wehia faced the blood family lord. She saluted the man with the sword.

"A legendary sword," Lord Vess observed. "I thought I recognized the fuller." And this time, real doubt had entered in the slight tremble of his voice.

Wehia didn't reply. Talkers were always distracted in a duel. Lord Vess was one of them. Instead, she focused on her breathing, feeling herself calm down slowly. Her feet stood firm. She was ready to fight. She stared unwaveringly at Vess while they circled one another. The watching women were silent. Gone were the goading and encouragement. Wehia felt the heat on her back and the fire filling her being. It was as if she carried the hopes of all the holdings, major and minor. She could bear the weight. Geri's belief in her, her love. The honor of all the holdings, all the forges.

Sheer belief sustained her.

Lord Vess yielded first to the silent pressure. He attacked first with his faith line sword and Wehia blocked it with Cold Steel. Cold Steel didn't break like Fire Heart. Its edge remained true.

"Why so quiet?" Lord Vess muttered. He was using his weight to force her into submission. She put all her strength into pushing him off. He took a few steps back and grinned approvingly. "You seem to have improved."

Wehia kept her mouth shut, keeping an eye on Vess. Was he leaning on his left foot? She circled him again. He rushed her again, his sword grinding against Cold Steel as she blocked him again with a quick counter. She fought the urge to run. The fear was back. The memory of her falling…the wound…roared back. She closed her eyes briefly, chasing the fear back.

For her family. For the border people. For…

For herself.

For herself and Geri.

Her foot shot out and kicked Vess. He stumbled and faltered a little while she backed away. Before he could raise his sword, she came at him, Cold Steel's tip aiming for his throat. His sword drew up and batted Cold Steel away. Vess was visibly panting.

For the man bullied by the soldiers.

Wehia attacked again, Cold Steel singing out in metallic voice. Vess parried. For a moment, it was a flurry of parries and counters as the two duelists battled for dominance. Wehia slipped on the ground and Vess grabbed the opportunity, seeing her fall as an opening.

She ducked away, cursing her clumsiness and the winter slush.

For Mariad's encampment, razed to nothing.

Wehia began another round of attacks, confidently countered by Vess. She knew that he was a competent swordsman and was not unafraid to show off. She let him parry and counter. He *was* showing off, too. He had an audience this time.

For Vex. Poor, foolish Vex.

Fury gripped her, lending her strength. She fought back, causing Vess to lift an eyebrow, as if surprised. Her arms were fast becoming sore. Her shoulder ached. She needed to win fast. Or else it would be back to nothing and everyone would suffer again.

For Geri.

For her amal.

Beloved.

With a shout, she pressed on, beating Vess back with a parry that would make her sword master proud of her. She kept on hitting out, swinging Cold Steel, until Vess was forced into a kneeling position.

For myself.

For myself.

Cold Steel's tip found Vess's soft throat. A lump bobbed as he tried to swallow.

"Do you yield?" Wehia asked, her voice hoarse now with exhaustion.

Vess didn't reply. The Council members shouted and yelled. He glanced at them and they fell into a brooding, sullen silence.

"Yield," Wehia said. "I have won." The tip of her sword, Lady Shana's sword, pressed gently on the soft skin.

"I…yield," Lord Vess said in a defeated tone.

"You will adhere to my conditions?" Wehia said. Her arms throbbed. She was going to hurt for a long time.

"Yes." Lord Vess nodded quietly. "Why don't you just kill me? That would solve—"

"Nothing. Killing you will solve nothing. There has already been bloodshed today. I will not add to that."

Armed forge women led Lord Vess and the Council members away. Wehia watched the lord's slouched back as the man walked into the Council Hall. They would draft the treaty later. Now she sagged against Cold Steel with relief, barely registering Geri hugging her and her mother and aunt saying, "Well done!"

The treaty was drafted in the presence of the watching forge women and the Council members. While the women signed the paper, the war stopped. The attacking border people put down their weapons. They camped close to the river.

Wehia signed because she was going to reforge the Council Sword. Her hand still shook due to exhaustion. She desperately wanted a long soak in the bath.

Rohana and Hadana signed because they were witnesses. The t'Doniyat holding was reinstated back to a swordmaking holding. Rohana's eyes gleamed with tears of joy. There was no shame. No more. Now they could make swords.

All the forge mistresses signed because the swordsmith holdings now had seats in the Council Hall, at the Assembly. Geri was chosen to speak for the t'Tolani, a position she accepted humbly. Only Wehia knew that her eyes shone at the announcement.

Overnight, the borders were now lifted. The border people could now live on any piece of land on Metakse. The proclamation went out the moment the treaty was finalized. Corwin and Falia grudgingly agreed to the new treaty. But for now, peace had returned.

The City let off fireworks to celebrate the treaty. Then as Wehia and Geri watched as they trudged back to the holding, weary of bone and eager to remove their armor, they saw the wish lanterns lift into the air, glowing pink and flickering. This time, they heralded joy and celebration, not war.

Wehia experienced a pang of sadness. Somewhere, there was still mourning. They had cleaned Vex's body and sent it back to Mariad's encampment in a proper coffin. She wished she could be there to comfort Mariad and Kes.

As the City regained its peace and began rebuilding, Wehia rested and only returned back to the Council Hall to retrieve the Council Sword. The forge women walked into the Hall with heads lifted high.

The Shrine priestesses censed the Council Sword and wrapped the fragments in soft, velvet cloth. The head priestess gently laid the bundle in Wehia's arms and blessed her with more incense and a prayer. Wehia strode back to the holding, accompanied by the t'Tolani and t'Doniyat women dressed in their colored robes. Incense wreathed her. People cheered, waving banners and handkerchiefs.

When Wehia entered the forge of the t'Tolani, more women greeted and blessed her. Geri beamed with joy. Rohana bowed at the sight of the Council Sword.

Reverently, Wehia laid the Sword on the table. She carefully unwrapped the cloth. The fragments shone under the forge's light. There was more incense, more chanting, more praying. It was a beautiful moment. Wehia knew she could do it. She felt it in her bones. She was ready now. She was strong. Her heart was steadfast.

"I will reforge the Sword at the start of the month of the Plow," she declared to the watching forge women. They cheered so loudly the roof of the forge shook.

CHAPTER 16

FOR THE MONTH of the Plow, Wehia reforged the Council Sword. Like Fire Heart, she melted the fragments, combining the molten solution with steel alloys. Hadana and Rohana watched as she labored at the tajam. The furnace roared like a fiery sky serpent. Pleased that the solution had solidified to a perfect rectangle, Wehia then proceeded to hammer it. And like with Fire Heart, she heated the nascent blade into a pulsating, orange glow, heat treating it so that it could be resilient. Then she quenched the blade in clean water and the hissing and the billowing cloud pleased her to no end.

Wehia made sure that she repeated the process several times until she was certain the sword was sufficiently tempered enough for the next stage of the reforging.

While the sword cooled and settled, she worked on the pommel and the cross guards. The Council Sword was a sword from the faith line, perhaps even the first of its kind, Fire Heart's and Cold Heart's direct kin. Their ancestress, like Lunes to the rest of Wehia's kin and family.

Geri gave her food and drink. Wehia rested, nibbling on Shoveltide sweetmeats already being sold in the winter markets. The dried fruit gave her the energy to continue working on the sword. Her dreams were of the dancing crane and the running dog as well as a soaring hawk, which Rohana said was the emblem of Yin's holding. The animals danced around her, swirling in a golden cone of light. When she woke, she knew she was on the right path.

Lady Narin t'Nolyat sent gifts to the t'Tolani household: eight bone daggers all polished until their edges shone and they looked as bright as the steel in the forge. Via her messenger, she conveyed her joyful congratulations to the reinstatement of the t'Doniyat holding as a swordmaking clan.

Wehia was touched at Narin's gesture. She caressed the sunburst symbol she had now made into a necklace. One day she would visit Mariad's encampment and pay her respects. When the reforging and another important thing she needed done were finished, she would return to the fens. Now she had to focus on reforging the Council Sword.

When she finally joined all the vital parts of the Council Sword together, the entire holding gathered to watch. It was such a significant historical moment: the rebirth of the Sword and the importance of peace in Metakse. This time, it meant true unification, not the misery of broken trust and promises.

Singing under her breath, Wehia welded the Sword. After welding and binding the parts together, she lifted the Sword up and everyone burst into song, dancing and drumming.

"I am not done yet," Wehia said softly.

Wehia polished and filed the sword until it gleamed. With a dry cloth, she rubbed away any smudge of oil.. The pommel and guards glistened. The blade…The blade seemed alive with light. In her mind, the hawk screamed and soared in a cloudless sky. Somewhere, she knew Yin smiled and Lady Shani happily approved of her task, beaming proudly.

"It's done," she said.

Yet it was not truly over when she slid the Council Sword into a scabbard she'd made for it. Made of hardwood with whorls of gold, the scabbard gleamed too as if with its own light.

The sound of the Council Sword sliding into the scabbard was satisfying. Wehia was relieved and happy. It also meant that she had crossed the threshold and that she still had to test it.

When the month of the Shovel finally arrived, Wehia subjected the Council Sword to a series of stress tests like she had with Fire Heart.

"It cuts like a hot knife through butter," Rohana observed, chuckling. "Knife, eh? We have made knives for far too long!"

Slicing it through a spring gourd, Wehia could see that the Council Sword was functional like any sword, any blade. She checked it for fractures and cracks. There were none. Once bitten, twice shy.

I am stronger now, Wehia thought. *Stronger, more resilient.*

She cut the gourds a few more times.

But I am not mature yet. I am strong. I still have a long way to go.

Geri approached her, smiling. Wehia's heart soared like the hawk in her dreams at the sight of the girl.

We will form our own forge eventually. Now's not the time.

"You look happy," Geri said.

"It's done," Wehia said. "It's finally done."

"Well done." Geri leaned close to kiss her on the cheek. Wehia laughed, the first happy laugh she had ever felt for years.

Wehia then faced Geri and held her amal's hands. "You know, I've meant to ask you something for a while now…"

With solemn ceremony, Wehia carried the sword up the Council Hall steps. Her kin lined the steps, throwing petals from spring flowers into the air. While the Shrine priestesses blessed the stand and the clean, red velvet drapes for the new Council Sword, Wehia smiled briefly at the Council members, who included representatives from both blood families and swordsmith holdings. Geri nodded with a twinkle in her eyes. The t'Tolani girl wore the blue of her holding and a green sash across her chest. All the swordsmith holding women in the Council wore green sashes.

At the bottom of the steps was a large crowd of City and border people, cheering and waving flags bearing the colors of the City. It was a riotous sea of red and yellow. Wehia caught sight of Mariad and Kes as they jostled with the people. Mariad looked sad, face downcast, while Kes was more overwhelmed, her eyes bewildered as if she were a skittish fen deer frightened by the noise and people. Wehia had been like that a long time ago. The girl caught sight of Wehia and waved meekly. Wehia nodded, smiling. She decided she would invite Kes to join Hadana's forge as an apprentice as well as to learn the ways of the sword. This was to signify a new start for both swordsmith holding and encampment. Hadana and her mother might have thoughts about this, but Wehia was confident things were going to change.

With a full heart, Wehia held the Council Sword aloft, Geri beside her, before placing the blade gently on the velvet drapes. Thunderous applause and cheering erupted from the watching crowds. It was done. The Sword had been reforged and returned to its rightful place.

At that exact moment, Wehia saw the name of the forge she would found in the future together with Geri seared bright in her mind. Her aunt and mother had already given them their blessings.

Amal.

Love.

Beaming, she turned to face the crowd.

Her heart was ready for anything.

THE END

ACKNOWLEDGEMENTS

Many people build a village and community. Forge women make the forge. This is so for the creation of a book. Here is an ever-growing list of thank yous.

To Lyssa Chiavari for all the hard work she has put in. And the many hours she has heard from me talking about *Fire Heart* and *Cold Steel*.

To Amy McNulty for the editing.

To Yasu Matsuoka for the beautiful cover illustrations.

To my readers.

And most of all, to my family, both blood and found. Your support is my strength.

You all keep the fire of the kilns burning and the signal fire shining.

METAKSE, A GUIDE

APPRENTICE

An apprentice trains under an experienced forge woman, often the forge mistress herself. They run errands and do the more menial tasks at the forge. An older apprentice seeking the rank of forge women would intend to make a weapon of her choice. Attainment of this rank (also applies to senior apprentices) is marked with riotous celebrations and food in the form of noodles with two eggs to symbolize fruitfulness. It varies, from holding to holding and at the discretion of the forge mistress, how apprentices are elevated to senior apprentices and forge women. Some senior apprentices serve as forge women in holdings that might require their assistance.

AMAL

A term of affection between two people. It means "dearest heart" or "love".

BARETTI PARROTS

Parrots known for their colorful plumage and loud squawking. They are popular as pets.

BOOK OF SWORDS

An important record kept by swordsmith archivists to keep track of the styles and kinds of blades and weapons made by the holding. A holding's book of swords records both its history and lineage.

BORDER
PEOPLE

Largely nomadic and itinerant groups of people. They often include individuals affected by poverty and loss. They literally live along the border between the fens and the sea. The City of Swords perceives the border people as ruffians and thieves.

BLOOD

The aristocratic families in the City of Swords are often called the blood or the blood families. They are members of the Council, which controls the political and economic interests of the land, holding frequent meetings and debates to decide on important matters of state. Certain blood families hold military power and organize the regiments who patrol the land.

CIDER

Often drunk warm during the winter months. It is made with either apples or pears.

DAGGER-COIN

A type of money used in Metakse. One dagger-coin is approximately worth one Metaksean dollar.

DOMMET
DRUMS

Light frame drums used by women in the swordsmith holdings. They are played during celebrations and festivals. The size of the drums vary. The ones used by the t'Doniyat are the size of handheld rice sifters.

FAMILIAL TERMS	**t':** prefix for clan. It means "the clan of …"
	ef: This suffix, placed after the names of an adopted female child or an apprentice, and before the clan name the child has joined. It means "belonging to…" For example, Wehia Jirin t'Doniyat *ef* t'Tolani and Geri Shaara *ef* t'Tolani.

Every girl child from the swordsmith holdings is given two names at birth. Her second name will be the name of her own household or holding, with its own forge. For example, if Wehia has her own holding, it will be called the t'Jirin holding and Wehia will then be called Wehia t'Jirin.

FEN	Or fens. The moor-like wide spaces, with straggly groves and frequently flooded and misty. The area south of the City is considered largely problematic with constant uprisings by the border people.
FEN PONY	A type of wild pony found in the fens. They are often domesticated for riding and to carry luggage. Fen ponies have thick brown or dun-colored coats that grow shaggy during winter.
ICE FISH	A fish species that live in the Verru river and thrive under ice. Their meat is thick and sweet.

INKS	Apart from its swords, Metakse is also famous for the inks produced by families who specialize in ink and dye production. The inks and dyes, made from plants from the outer islands, are highly pigmented, expensive but of excellent quality. Many swordsmith holdings use such inks for their books of swords. Examples of these inks are Verusian black and Jessian silver.
JESSIAN	The name of a special silver-hued ink derived from jess, a kind of plant found on the outer islands. The plant's stems produce the distinctive silver color beloved by inkmakers and swordsmith holding archivists. The stem of the jess plant is also mildly toxic and must be harvested while wearing thick gloves.
LANGUAGE	The people of Metakse speak a common tongue, called Askan, which means "language".
MORA PASTE	Also called 'mora', this is a reddish spicy paste eaten with food. Each family has their own recipe for the paste.
MORANI STEW	Eaten all year around, this is a soupy stew made with meat, vegetables and tubers, and is best eaten with hot bread or river rice. Each family has their own version.

MOON COOKIES	A delicious sweet treat and dessert. Crescent-shaped, they are feather-light and dusted with powdery sugar.
PROMISE RINGS	Given to a loved one. They are not betrothal rings.
QIMAAT	A board game, rather like chess, played by two people.
RACE	Metakse is monoethnic, but not mono-cultural, as regional variations have developed in food, music, dress and other customs and practices.
RELIGION	The Sword Goddess is worshiped in her Shrine in the City of Swords. She is the patron of young lovers, young women and swordsmiths, but all seek her protection. The Goddess's feast days occur in the months of the Shovel, the Flint, and the Saber. Offerings include white candles, small swords, daggers, ores, shovels, and tiny trinkets made of steel and silver.
RIVER RICE	A type of grain growing wild in rivers and streams. It is also cultivated commercially.
SHOVEL-TIDE	New year celebrations. It is celebrated with gift-giving. Popular gifts are necklaces and bracelets, and other trinkets.

SOOKEE	Popular beverage made from nuts. Thick and sweet, it is drunk topped with fresh whipped cream as a treat. It is also drunk as a breakfast drink. Some people prefer it unsweetened.
SIGNAL FIRE	Maintained by women trained with knowledge of chemistry, the signal fire burns constantly like a beacon at the top of the main building of a holding. Different colors symbolize different things. Blue means that a message is on its way; green stands for peace; red, danger.
STEAM	Most of the holdings and the aristocratic blood families run on steam. Steam generates energy for amenities like hot water, heat and lighting. Councilors have debated the use of steam as burning of coal pollutes the air.
STOLATI HUMMERS	Tiny birds that resemble hummingbirds. They feed on flower nectar and make tiny cup-like nests. Their feathers shimmer in metallic tones.
SUNBURST	A sun-shaped talisman made with dry brush, wires or hair.
SWORDSMITH HOLDING	Matriarchal and matrilineal clan born and trained to make specific or specialized blades or steel objects. The skills are passed from mother to daughter or from aunt to niece.

TAJAM   Furnace used in the making of gem steel.

TOFFEE FRUIT   Fruits dipped in toffee, a street food sold in
                        the City throughout the Metakse year. The
                        overall texture is crunchy on the outside and
                        soft inside.

VERRU (RIVER)   An important river that runs through and
                        bisects the City of Swords. Deep and dark-
                        colored (because of black silt), this river
                        serves as a transportation route and a vital
                        source of food and water. It ends at a delta
                        close to the southeast coast.

VERU   A plant, found in the outer islands, used to
                        make the famous Verusian Black ink. The
                        name comes from the word "ver", which
                        means black or dark.

WRAP   Worn by the women in some swordsmith
                        holdings. The t'Doniyat are known to wear
                        distinctive wraps of dyed textiles woven with
                        vivid patterns.

WEEKS &   A week comprises eight days and is called an
DAYS   eight-day. The days do not have names and
                        are simply referred to as First, Second, Third,
                        etc.

XYLIA

A type of plant found in some parts of the colder fen regions closer to the mountain ridges. It is actually a type of grass with a shiny but resilient "bark" and hollow stem. Used by the mountain people as food and kitchenware. Also used by the swordsmith holdings to test their blades. Pronounced SEE-lia.

MONTHS OF THE METAKSE YEAR

SHOVEL — The first month of spring. Celebration of spring. Shovel-tide marks the celebration of spring.

HAMMER — Mid-spring. Families commission weapons as gifts or for their own use. People use this time to do repairs of houses and holdings.

SICKLE — The last month of spring. Novice-taking takes place during this month. Early produce is harvested.

DAGGER — The first month of summer. Harvesting begins. City folk begin celebration of marriages and parties.

AXE — Mid-summer. Harvesting. Skinning of livestock. Celebration of marriages and parties.

SCYTHE — The last month of summer. Harvesting and skinning continues. Waxing of meats and making of sausages begin. The number of commissions traditionally drops around this period, though City and fen holdings are kept busy with two or three medium-to-big projects normally commissioned by wealthy families.

FLINT   The first month of autumn. The Feast of the
                    Flint. People celebrate with sausages. Farmers
                    begin weaning the young of their livestock.
                    Sausages and waxed meats are stored in
                    preparation for the winter months. Birds and
                    animals begin fattening up and start their
                    hibernation. Nest-building slows down and
                    stops. Farmers till and plow their fields.

HOOK   Mid-autumn. Farmers begin to house their
                    animals indoors in preparation for winter.
                    Repair of heaters. Stocking up on wood and
                    coal.

SWORD   The last month of autumn. Farmers sell rams
                    and other male livestock at the markets.

KNIFE   First month of winter. Forge women do their
                    stock-taking and inventory. Last-minute
                    commissions are completed. Around this time,
                    the holdings stop taking in commissions.

SABER   Mid-winter. Stock-taking. Hummers hibernate.
                    Plants are more or less bare.

PLOW   The last month of winter. Month of planning
                    for the coming year. Winter plowing continues.

ABOUT THE AUTHOR

Joyce Ch'ng lives in Singapore. They write science fiction and fantasy as well as YA and MG. Their short stories have appeared in *The Apex Book of World SF II*, *The Future Fire* and *Multispecies Cities*. *Dragon Dancer* (Lantana Publishing) is Joyce's first picture book, celebrating dragon dancing and Lunar New Year; it was followed by *Oyster Girl* (Pepper Dog Press), a tribute to their grandmother and the hawker heritage in Singapore. For YA readers, *Fire Heart* is a fantasy book about swords and coming-of-age. You can find Joyce at their website (awolfstale.wordpress.com), or on X and Bluesky at @jolantru.